Love
and
Other
Recreational
Sports

Love

and

Other

Recreational

Sports

John Dearie

Viking

VIKING
Published by the Penguin Group
Penguin Putnam Inc., 375 Hudson Street, New York, New York 10014, U.S.A.
Penguin Books Ltd, 80 Strand, London WC2R 0RL, England
Penguin Books Australia Ltd, 250 Camberwell Road, Camberwell,
    Victoria 3124, Australia
Penguin Books Canada Ltd, 10 Alcorn Avenue,
    Toronto, Ontario, Canada M4V 3B2
Penguin Books India (P) Ltd, 11 Community Centre, Panchsheel Park,
    New Delhi – 110 017, India
Penguin Books (N.Z.) Ltd, Cnr Rosedale and Airborne Roads, Albany,
    Auckland, New Zealand
Penguin Books (South Africa) (Pty) Ltd, 24 Sturdee Avenue,
    Rosebank, Johannesburg 2196, South Africa

Penguin Books Ltd, Registered Offices:
80 Strand, London WC2R 0RL, England

First published in 2003 by Viking Penguin,
a member of Penguin Group (USA) Inc.

10 9 8 7 6 5 4 3 2 1

PUBLISHER'S NOTE
This is a work of fiction. Names, characters, places, and incidents either are the product of the author's imagination or are used fictitiously, and any resemblance to actual persons, living or dead, business establishments, events, or locales is entirely coincidental.

Grateful acknowledgment is made for permission to reprint an excerpt from "Understand Your Man" by Johnny R. Cash. © 1964 (renewed) Chappell & Co. All rights reserved. Used by permission of Warner Bros. Publications U.S. Inc., Miami, Florida.

LIBRARY OF CONGRESS CATALOGING-IN-PUBLICATION DATA
Dearie, John.
    Love and other recreational sports / by John Dearie,
        p.   cm.
    ISBN 0-670-03219-0
    1. Dating (Social customs)—Fiction.   2. Young men—Fiction.   I. Title.

    PS3604.E455 L6 2003
    813'.6—dc21   2002032418

This book is printed on acid-free paper. ∞
Printed in the United States of America
Set in Aldus with Nueva display

This book is dedicated to New York City,

my city,

where the sidewalks are stages, the subways are concert halls,

and the people, my neighbors, are brave and true.

The Lord God said, "It is not good for the man to be alone. I will make a suitable helper for him."
—Genesis 2:18

I was within and without, simultaneously enchanted and repelled by the inexhaustible variety of life.
—F. Scott Fitzgerald, *The Great Gatsby*

Acknowledgments

One of the strange things about writing a book—one of the many—is that, while the act of converting concept to words on a page is utterly solitary, carried out in quiet, lonely rooms (or the shower, or the subway, or a bar, or lying in bed at night), getting the finished product into readers' hands requires the support and assistance of a small army. My sincere thanks to those who took an interest in this project and who provided critical assistance along the way.

To my readers: my parents, John and Madelaine Dearie; Jennifer Eatz; Sarah Wean; John P. "Jack" Dearie (who should do some writing himself); Jim and Carol West; Bill and Carol Istock; Paul Lilly; Brian Boyle; Chris Calabia and Suzanne Brown; Dianne Dobbeck; Justin Daly; Linda Dallas Rich; George Peng; Caroline Wittenberg; and Granville Martin. Thanks to all for the gifts of their time and honest input.

To Pam Dorman and Ann Mah at Viking: many thanks for taking a chance on a new writer, for your kind delivery of insightful comments, and for helping to make this book the best it could be.

What can a writer say about an agent who not only thinks enough of your book that she wants to represent it, but who also takes the time and care to make discerning suggestions you wish you had thought of yourself, and who, ultimately, lands you a contract with Viking? Profound thanks to Alice Martell, my partner and friend, and to her wonderful assistant, Stephanie Finman.

Special thanks to Lance Auer and Jet Auer de Saram. Without their enormous generosity this book might never have been written.

And, finally, to my wife, Stefanie. We learned that the book had been purchased while in Spain on our honeymoon, which was only appropriate. As tormenting and grueling as writing a novel can sometimes be, I think that in many ways the person who loves the writer carries the greatest burden. Thank you, sweetheart, for putting up with the hundreds of hours away. My pensive, distracted moods. My frustrations and tantrums. Your love and reassurance are my inspiration and refuge. This is our victory.

Love
and
Other
Recreational
Sports

Chapter 1

Tom. Married.

I still couldn't believe it. I simply couldn't believe it was really going to happen.

I tried again. Tom . . . *married*?

With a helpless sigh, I closed my eyes and slowly, gently, shook my aching head. I could scarcely fathom the notion. And it had nothing to do with my alcohol-impaired condition. In the three years that we were roommates, Tom never had a girlfriend. Never even tried to have one. Never seemed particularly interested.

It was all very strange: in recent years, my college friends had been tying the knot in something of a reverse logical order—those who, for whatever reason, rarely if ever dated dropping off first; those of us who seemed always to be in a relationship still flying the flag, more than a decade later.

Rolling over, I groped for the phone; finally finding it, I dialed Alex's number. "You bringing a date to this thing?"

"A *date?*" he laughed. "Dude, you don't bring sand to the beach."

Alex frequently spoke in code—short, pithy phrases meant as oddly poetic revelations of some higher truth. Maybe that's why he was in advertising. Usually I understood, but that morning, newly awake and badly hung over, I was slow on the uptake. The wedding was nowhere near a beach.

"What are you talking about?" I said, nauseous, in pain, and with no patience for rhetorical riddles.

"It's a *wedding,* Jack," he said, as if I were missing the obvious. "Target-rich environment. The single friends of the happy couple. The women. Weddings make them crazy. Tick-tock, tick-tock, right?" Again the lascivious chuckle. "Like shooting fish in a barrel."

. . .

I was in the wedding party, so I had to drive out to New Jersey for the rehearsal that evening. The bride, Michelle, was from Passaic, less than an hour away, right over the George Washington Bridge. Even so, I passed on the more logical option of a quick and cheap bus ride and decided to rent a car instead. A car-deprived Manhattanite, I jumped at any excuse to get behind the wheel and hit the road.

Alex decided to come along. He wasn't in the wedding, but other friends from college were flying in that night and he knew a ruckus was likely. I remember wishing I had thought of that before I had embalmed myself the night before.

As we crossed the bridge, Manhattan's spectacular hulk stretching south over our left shoulder, Alex said: "So, you ready, dude? You psyched?"

The other quirky feature of the strange language Alex

spoke was his penchant for the word "dude." We all knew he meant it as a term of endearment, like "buddy" or "pal," or Gatsby's "old sport." Or to convey the gravity of what he was about to say—the way the Gospels have Jesus beginning particularly important pronouncements with: "Amen, I say to you," or "I solemnly assure you. . . ." But "dude" was a word that I and the rest of my friends had discarded years before, a dated accessory, like a red power tie, that just didn't work for a man of thirty-five. And he used it with such frequency that it sometimes became a distraction, a kind of rhetorical tic—the way some people (mostly women in my experience) can't get through, like, a sentence without, you know, like, dropping the word "like," like, every three or four words. Even so, it was an aspect of Alex's persona I couldn't imagine him without; one that oddly complemented his wiry, slump-shouldered frame, his unruly hair, and the happy smirk into which his boyish features seemed naturally and permanently twisted.

"Am I psyched for what?" I asked.

"For meeting desperate, horny women."

I frowned. "I've given up women."

"Oh, come on," he groaned.

"Women and alcohol. They cost too damn much and are more trouble than they're worth."

"Don't let one nutty chick screw up your head."

"She was only the latest."

"So what then, you've gone gay?"

"That's right," I said. "A dry, celibate gay man."

"You won't last."

"Watch me."

. . .

I hadn't gone out the night before with the intention of drinking. Not as much as I did, anyway. I had, of course, planned on a couple. I needed them.

Since Kim and I had split, friends had been setting me up with every un-spoken-for they could think of—friends, friends of friends, sisters and co-workers of friends of friends. That evening it was Sam, as in Samantha. Alex had repeated her name over and over with lecherous delight: "Samanthaaaa-ha-ha-ha. . . ."

We'd met for dinner at a new *tapas* place over on Second Avenue. Nice enough girl. Smart and attractive. A copy editor at *Travel & Leisure* magazine. Things proceeded in the jumpy, awkward way that first dates tend to go. At one point, Sam said, "Do you know that for every inch taller someone is they use, like, *hundreds* of gallons more water each year and require far more oxygen than the average person?"

I took a moment or two to ponder this revelation, then said, "So basketball players are bad for the environment?"

"Oh, very, *very* bad," she said. No wink, no tight-lipped smirk.

Under normal circumstances I might have been able to hang with it. But, as it was, my head just wasn't in the game. Since the break-up, dating had been an insufferable chore, like forcing down a meal after a harrowing bout of food poisoning—the slightest whiff of romantic intrigue would send me reeling. It had, in fact, become so difficult that I couldn't do it without a little lubrication beforehand—a quick scotch and soda, a glass or two of wine.

You might wonder why I had conceded to such torture. If dating was so unpleasant, so awful, why bother? Well, because my friends had insisted—a view more or less in line with my own assessment of things—that I shouldn't sit at home pining away like a driveling sap. I needed to get back on my feet, back in the saddle. And with a fierce enthusiasm. A vengeance. Meeting new people, successfully dating, and, hopefully, some easy, hassle-free sex was the best treatment for the blow I'd sustained. And so I had found myself in the absurd position of being firmly committed to a course of action that I simply couldn't execute while cold sober.

But what had really done me in the night before was the question Sam asked about twenty minutes into our conversation. Our first round of *tapas* had just arrived. As my fork sliced into the shrimp paella, she looked across the table, smiled cheerfully, and said: "So, you published yet?"

Sam had been well briefed. Most of my friends knew that I wrote in my spare time, which was scarce given the seventy hours a week routinely demanded by the bank for which I helped structure mergers and acquisitions. But I had persevered: working, training, hoping. For years I'd dreamed of quitting the staid, antiseptic world of numbers and ratios for the rich, full-nostriled, creative existence of the successful writer.

And I liked to think I had the aptitude. I'd always been a voyeur of sorts, had an eye for story, and was a proficient builder of sentences—which is to say that mine were as competent as those crafted by any of the wildly popular writers whose work I had consulted. Of midwestern extraction and possessing, I suppose, the region's sensibility for the practical, I am not by nature one of those prone to deluding themselves about their abilities; if I'm simply not cut out for something, I have no interest in torturing myself.

But I wanted to write and it seemed to me that, given my particular abilities, the ambition was a reasonable one. I'd never studied writing—I was an economics major, naturally—but then, as Truman Capote once observed: one either is or is not a writer, and no combination of professors can influence the outcome. I'd had an idea for a novel for some time, but so far had focused on short stories—practicing the craft, honing my skills, searching for my own distinctive style.

Sam had meant no harm. In fact, I knew her question was meant as something of a joke—a playful way of inquiring, quite politely, about my writing, something she'd been told was important to me. What she didn't and couldn't have known is that I absolutely despised the question. And for several reasons.

For one thing, I was not, as yet, published and, like most *as yet* unpublished writers, I didn't enjoy being reminded of that torturous fact. I'd had the distinct pleasure and high honor of having stories of mine rejected by some of the most prestigious magazines in the country, but the thrill was decidedly short-lived.

Furthermore, "So, you published yet?" seemed to assert that you weren't a real writer until your work had, in fact, been published—duly validated by the commercial marketplace. Now, don't get me wrong; as a good capitalist, I had no problem with the marketplace and would have celebrated wildly even a little commercial validation. What I did mind, though, was the suggestion, however subtly or inadvertently made, that the many months I spent toiling over a story had no value whatsoever *unless* the resulting property was acquired, printed, and released to the warm embrace of the reading and paying masses.

Worst of all was the grating tenor of the question, the poking expectation—the lurking condescension. "So, you published yet?" seemed to say that if you were any kind of writer at all, if you had the slightest modicum of talent, if you were merely capable of lining up words in a way that was even vaguely comprehensible, you would be published. If only that were true. Reality, I'm afraid, is both more complicated and more dreadful: I recently read an article in which a noted editor put the odds of a new writer finishing a novel, landing an agent, and getting published at one in ten thousand.

I mention all this not to make excuses (not really, anyway), but only to explain that when Sam quite innocently and even kindly asked, "So, you published yet?" the displeasure of the already unpleasant situation was ratcheted considerably. After gritting my teeth through my pat "still working on a few things" reply, it seemed the only reasonable thing to do was to get properly smashed. But, alas, escape is but an illusion, and ultimately self-defeating. Intoxication, as I had learned, whether emotional or chemical, demands its price.

And so that morning, as I suffered through the roiling aftermath of yet another blurry, failed encounter, it finally dawned on me that what I really needed, on both fronts, was a period of abstinence. Purification. Detox.

That, I finally realized, was the only healthy thing to do, and a course to which I could commit. And stick.

Chapter 2

I'd never met Michelle. Neither had Alex. She and Tom worked in Chicago and the courtship had been quick, just under a year. This only heightened the strangeness of what was about to happen: not only was Tom getting married, he was marrying a total stranger. Having no one to picture him with in my mind, I couldn't even begin to get used to the idea. The whole situation had me nauseous.

The drive out somehow helped. That and the liter of water I drank in the car. I arrived in Passaic feeling almost human.

We swung by the hotel to check in, drop our stuff, and make a pit stop, then headed over to the church. We arrived twenty minutes late.

Tom was standing on the front steps with his parents and two other people. He greeted us warmly, reminded his parents who we were, and introduced Father George—mid-forties, pleasantly plump, kind face, salt-and-pepper hair. Then Tom took the hand of the woman standing beside him.

"Guys," he said, in a tone of soft affection I had never heard from him, "this is Michelle."

"Very nice to finally meet you," I said as we shook hands. Michelle was petite and plain; unremarkable features, shoulder-length brown hair. The word "mousy" came to mind. So did the word "Catholic."

"Likewise," she said, smiling stiffly. "Everyone else is inside."

I nodded obediently and headed into the church. "She's miffed we're late," I whispered to Alex.

"Yep."

I'd often wondered what kind of woman Tom would marry, assuming he ever did. My curiosity stemmed in part from his seeming lack of interest in women. In college he would dutifully find a date for dances or other big events the rest of us were going to, but otherwise never made a serious effort to connect. We never doubted his inclinations; Tom was quiet, somewhat awkward, not particularly attractive—short and rather thickly built, balding, his nose a bit too long, his blue eyes set a bit too far apart—and we figured he just wasn't terribly adept at or comfortable with what the successful pursuit of women required. We also figured that he was probably still a virgin.

And he had always been very Catholic. Catholicism, of course, isn't like pregnancy—it's not a you-is-or-you-ain't sort of thing. There's a spectrum, a sliding scale from absurdly permissive to absurdly repressive. I was more liberal, whereas Tom had always been, for my money anyway, awfully conservative. He and I had locked horns more than once over the years, and on all the typical topics—from birth control and homosexuality to the male-only priesthood and papal infallibility. Alex, a devoutly nominal Protestant, would sometimes watch the argument, beer in hand, his head turning left and right, as if he were enjoying a tennis match. Given Tom's views, I'd sometimes wondered if he'd ever find anyone.

And so my immediate reaction to Michelle didn't surprise me. She reminded me of my mother. Or a nun. It was her plain, unremarkable features. Her mousy hair. The disapproving look in her flat eyes as she shook my hand. Still, I felt bad about my appraisal. We *were* late, after all, and I'd only known the woman for two minutes.

Half an hour later, I sat in the second pew next to Alex watching Tom and Michelle walk through the next day's ceremony with Father George. Leaning over, I whispered, "So what do you think of Michelle?"

Alex folded his arms across his chest. He studied Michelle, just a few yards away, his eyes narrowing as he pondered my query. After several moments of careful consideration, he leaned toward me: "He'll never get her doggy."

• • •

The rehearsal dinner was pleasant if typically banal—prime rib followed by silly toasts from family and friends. The wine looked delicious, but I stuck to iced tea.

I arrived back at the hotel just before nine o'clock. Walking through the lobby, I heard a tremendous racket coming from the bar. It took a moment, but then I knew. Swinging open the door, I was greeted by a cheer from friends I hadn't seen in five years. The air inside was close with cigarette smoke and shouted conversations, warm with tightly packed bodies and laughter. Pounds had been gained, hair lost or graying, but all in all everyone looked terrific. My floundering spirits were instantly lifted.

By midnight the bar was dark, my friends lit. We had taken over the place, having frightened off other guests. True to my pledge, I sipped ginger ale.

"Okay, *listen!*" a friend named Gina suddenly shouted from the end of the table. I could tell she was drunk because she was smoking, something she generally didn't do; living in Boston, she'd run the marathon twice. We all reluctantly quieted.

"Okay, so a few hours after creating Adam," Gina began, "God says to him, 'All right, look, Adam, I like you. I like you a lot. You're my most precious creation. Made in my own image and likeness. And because I like you so much, I've decided to give you a couple of things that will distinguish you from all my other creations.'

"'Like what?' Adam says.

"'Well,' God answers, 'like I've given you the largest brain of all my creations.'

"'That's great,' says Adam. 'Thanks, God. Anything else?'"

We were all grinning now; we knew what was coming.

"'Well, yes,' God says. 'I've also given you the largest penis of all my creations.'"

"That's *not* true," another friend, Anne, said suddenly.

"Yes, it is," Gina insisted, annoyed that her patter had been interrupted.

"Horses? Elephants?" Anne offered. "Haven't you ever been to the zoo?" This set off a series of knowing looks and nods of genuine wonder among the women.

"*Proportionately,*" I threw out, knowing Gina would never come up with it.

"Exactly," she said. "Thank you, Jack." Then turning to Anne: "Now *shut up!*"

Laughter.

Turning back to the rest of us, she hesitated: "Damn it, now I forget where I was."

"Largest brain and penis," we all said.

"Oh, right. So Adam says, 'Cool. Thanks, God.'

"But then God says, 'There's just one catch.'

"'Yeah, what's that?' Adam asks.

"And God says, 'I've only given you enough blood to use one at a time.'"

The women roared. The men laughed too, but with a kind of grudging resignation.

Ah, dick jokes. That most reliable and satisfying subgenre of sexual humor. As I watched my drunken friends cough with laughter, from my sober vantage point I wondered for a moment about the nature of the dick joke and the source of its nearly universal appeal.

The very fact that there are dick jokes implies that the penis is something to joke about. There aren't many vagina jokes. The vagina just isn't very funny. There are boob jokes, but it's not the same. No, it occurred to me that there must be something essentially comical, or comically absurd, or maybe just absurd, about the penis.

I was aware that some women find the penis funny on at least one level. As a female friend once explained: "Well, because you've got this . . . *thing*! This extra part! Right in front! That's so *weird!*" she said, absently grabbing at her pubic area with both hands. "I can't even imagine what that's like. I mean, doesn't it, like, get in the way?"

"I guess you get used to it," I'd answered. "Like having something in your eye."

"But it's not in your *eye*!" she shrieked. "It's right *there*! In front! This little handle! This fun little hose! And it does tricks," she said, her eyes widening. "It gets big, and then small again. Sometimes *really* small. Shrinkage!" she squealed, imitating *Seinfeld*'s George Costanza. "I mean, it's like you have this living thing, this *creature* in your pants!"

Creature. Implying something independent, something foreign. Even menacing.

Which, it occurred to me, is getting close to what really makes dick jokes funny. Namely, that penises are attached to men, who are forever condemned to live and come to terms with this thing, this creature, in their pants. A creature that, at times, seems to have its own agenda, its own priorities—a veritable mind of its own. A mind that too often seems at odds with the best interests of the man it's attached to.

Which brought me, at last, to the essential core of the matter, the universal truth that dick jokes, in all their graphic glory, so comically reveal. It is, of course, that men sometimes do odd, illogical, or even incredibly stupid things because of their penises, as if . . . well, indeed, as if the blood had suddenly drained from their skulls, causing their oxygen-deprived brains to shut down.

I concluded that women like dick jokes because they tag men as incorrigible idiots, while men like dick jokes because they imply that, as hapless slaves to their biology, men simply can't be blamed for being incorrigible idiots.

Later, with the hour growing late and energy levels waning, the crowd had divided by gender: men around one table, women around another. Within minutes the subject around the male table turned to sex; it had been a long while since we'd last seen each other and there was catching up to do, stories to be swapped.

At one point, a friend held the rest of us positively rapt with his telling of how, six months before, he had scored the Holy Grail of male sexual fantasies—Two Women at the Same Time. "Roommates," he said.

Heads were slowly shaken, homage paid.

Wide-eyed and grinning, our minds piqued with prurient fascination, hunched forward so as not to miss a single deliciously sordid detail, we listened in utter, stupefied silence to this real-life *Penthouse* "Forum" column, this toe-curling tale that every one of us had dreamed about but never expected to actually achieve. Not a sip of beer was taken in over ten minutes.

And then he really blew us away: "So there we were," he said. "Me and these two gorgeous, bisexual roommates, crawling all over each other, right?"

We all nodded, transfixed.

"And then guess what happens," he said, suddenly grim. "Or *doesn't*."

A momentary pause; then a dozen faces collapsed, mouths dropped open.

"No," Alex groaned in horror. "*No!*"

Our friend nodded, frowning miserably: "Droopy Snoopy."

"*Aaaaahhhhhhh!*" we cried in collective agony.

On the verge of bagging the ultimate trophy, with the coveted, twin-headed, twice-willing, double-your-pleasure prey lined up blond, glistening, and panting in the crosshairs, our friend's otherwise reliable and enthusiastic member—the creature—overwhelmed by the enormity of his good fortune, suddenly, tragically, decided to opt out.

Together we all mourned. It was as if he'd told us he had terminal cancer.

· · ·

The wedding was to begin at eleven A.M. By nine-thirty I was up, dressed, finished with breakfast, and ready to go. Returning to the hotel room, I found Alex just lumbering into the shower. "Alex, I cannot be late! I'm leaving in ten minutes!"

"Not a problem, dude!" he called from behind the curtain. He finished dressing in the car.

The weather had obliged: a beautiful late-summer day, clear and bright, warm but with low humidity, which, for whatever reason, always seems to make the colors of the world—the sky, the leaves, cars and houses and everything else—appear sharper, more brilliant, more lovely. The church was small and quaint, looking more Lutheran or Presbyterian than Catholic—stacked sandstone blocks topped with a charming bell tower, typical of New Jersey's leafy northern suburbs.

Inside, guests were already arriving. Free of ushering duties—Tom's two brothers and a cousin did the honors—I huddled with the other groomsmen near the altar. Forgetting where we were, we furtively scoped the arriving female guests, debating with our eyes and facial expressions who was attractive and who appeared to be single.

Finally, we got the signal: Michelle had arrived.

Looking toward the back of the church, through the lavender taffeta of the bridesmaids, I caught sight of a person-sized puff of white, as if a giant cotton ball or snowflake had blown in the front door.

Tom joined us with his brother Mike, the best man. Our tuxedos were identical, except Tom's bow tie was white. We retreated to the sacristy, to the right of the altar—just offstage. The room was small and stuffy. Father George had just finished dressing. His vestments were white, green, and yellow—colors of celebration, optimism, renewal. "So, are we ready?" he asked with an easy grin.

Tom heaved a heavy, nervous sigh. "As ready as I'll ever be."

"Your last chance to make a break for it," Father said.

We all laughed. It was funny, especially coming from a priest. But as we laughed, I noticed that Father George didn't. He wasn't even chuckling. He still wore the same easy, priestly grin, but his eyes were steady and ardent; they held Tom in a sharp, appraising gaze. I suddenly realized he wasn't joking. He was asking Tom a serious question: Are you really ready? he wanted to know. Are you sure?

Tom seemed to understand. He nodded, his lips pressed tightly together. I wasn't sure if their pressing implied clear-eyed certainty or merely Tom's steely resolve to force himself to go through with it. Whatever it was, it seemed to satisfy Father.

"When you hear the music," he said, "that's your cue."

With that, he left and we were alone. Friends. Men. Friends of a man about to pledge the rest of his life to one woman. No matter what you think of the idea, it's an awesome moment. You sense it. Feel it. As if the infinite energy of the universe has suddenly focused on that tiny, stuffy room in Passaic, New Jersey.

I wanted to say something to my friend. Something appropriate, something profound. Nothing came to mind.

Someone said, "Wow," and we all chuckled knowingly, nodding our heads.

Tom thanked us for standing up for him. He shook our hands. Then, turning toward a nearby counter, he retrieved a series of small blue boxes I'd only just noticed. He tossed one at each of us. "Open them."

We each pulled from the tissue paper inside a silver-plated hip flask, our initials etched in large, ornate lettering on the front. We smiled and grunted approvingly.

"They're heavy," someone said.

Tom grinned. "They're full."

We spent the last few moments of Tom's life as a single man doing shots in the sacristy. My no-alcohol pledge was the furthest thing from my mind.

. . .

One after the other, the maid of honor (I've never thought "maid" sounded particularly honorable) and the four bridesmaids proceeded down the aisle. Then, as the music crescendoed, Michelle began her slow trek toward the altar and the rest of her life with Tom. Her father was puffed up like a rooster at her side. The guests stood; flashbulbs popped.

As they drew near, I saw that Michelle's father was now a wreck, tears streaming down his lined face. Tom met them at the foot of the altar. With trembling hands, Michelle's father lifted her veil, kissed his daughter once, and then again. Turning, he shook Tom's hand—I wondered if he could smell the whiskey on Tom's breath—then joined the hand with Michelle's. The custom, however primitive or patronizing, always brings a catch to my throat. Still overcome, the old man squeezed into the front pew beside his wife. She was solid as a rock and, grinning serenely, nestled him against her shoulder.

Father George welcomed the dearly beloved and began the Mass. We stood. We sat. We stood. We sat again. Friends mounted the lectern and read from scripture. We heard that love is patient and kind. That it is not boastful or profane. That the love between a man and a woman is holy because it is a reflection of God's boundless and enduring love for us all.

Finally it was time: Tom and Michelle stood to take their vows. The wedding party also stood. Michelle's sister was busy on the floor behind her, fluffing and straightening the train of her dress. From my vantage point, about ten feet to Tom's left, I had an unobstructed view of Michelle: her dress was simple but elegant; she wore makeup, but the colors were muted and tastefully done; her brown hair was artfully swirled and pinned atop her head, like that of a princess. She was beautiful, in the way that all brides are.

And for a moment I actually envied Tom. His search was over. He'd found her.

Suddenly, out of nowhere, Alex's comment invaded my mind. As I watched Michelle recite her vows, flush-cheeked and teary-eyed, her delicate voice quivering with love and emotion, I couldn't get the term "doggy-style" out of my head.

· · ·

The reception was at a nearby country club. Large round room, small round tables. Open bar, dinner for 150. Michelle's parents must have dropped a fortune.

Events proceeded as a virtual replay of the evening before:

salad, followed by prime rib or fish, followed by cake or fruit, followed by toasts and speeches. Tom and Michelle cut the cake for the official photographer and posterity, but mercifully dispensed with the bouquet and garter routine.

Finally the lights dimmed; a mirror ball began to twirl over the dance floor. A deejay spun a bizarre collage of tasteful standards by Frank and Tony and Ella, mixed in with the sadly de rigueur, like "Celebration" and "Get Down Tonight" and, strangest of all, given the occasion, Gloria Gaynor's anthem for jilted women, "I Will Survive."

Having refreshed my soda at the bar, I stood alone for a few moments surveying the scene. Looking around the enormous room, quietly observing the interaction of the guests, especially the single women, I did, in fact, sense, smell, a certain desperation. After all, most weren't just single and female, they were single, female, and Catholic—a triple whammy if there ever was one.

Out on the dance floor, Alex seemed to have made a connection: one of the bridesmaids—a blonde with impressive, amply displayed breasts. They'd been dancing together most of the evening. Watching them laugh and grope, I felt genuine pity for her.

Then, suddenly: "Hello."

I turned to find an attractive woman, tall and brunette, late twenties, standing next to me at the bar. "Hi," I said, rather unable to conceal my surprise.

"White wine," she said to the bartender. Presented with her drink, she turned back to me. "I'm Sarah Mitchell," she said pleasantly. "High school friend of the bride."

"Jack Lafferty," I said, taking her extended hand. "College friend of the groom."

Sarah smiled. "You look lonely over here."

"I do?"

She nodded, her eyes wide and hopeful.

I shrugged. "Just taking in the happy scene."

"Thinking about a story?"

"Sorry?"

"I hear you're a writer."

I frowned inwardly; Sarah had done her research, which implied intent. "A writer wanna-be," I said. "At the moment, I'm still just a banker."

"I know the feeling," she said, turning to face the room. "I'm a musician masquerading as a lawyer."

"Really?" I said, suddenly intrigued. "What do you play?"

"Guitar. Mostly acoustic. Classical." She looked back at me, her lips pursing slyly. "But I do own a Fender."

"You're kidding," I laughed.

"That surprises you?"

"A little," I admitted. "Not sure why."

An eyebrow arched. "Girls are supposed to play the piano or flute, right?"

"Something like that."

"My mother thinks so too." Another tight grin.

From the dance floor I suddenly recognized the opening synthesized chords of George Michael's "Freedom." A cheer went up as people pulled partners onto the floor.

"You know," Sarah said, setting her half-full glass on the bar behind us, "I haven't seen you dance yet."

"That's a good thing, I assure you."

"Oh, c'mon. On a floor that crowded," she said, indicating the now pulsing mob across the room, "no one cares what you look like."

Turning, I looked at her, really, for the first time: a soft oval face assembling generally smallish features—short nose, thinnish lips, a strong but gentle chin—which, pleasantly arranged, gave her a look of refinement despite the trace of freckles sprinkled across the bridge of her nose—the faint remains of a childhood spent in the sun. Most striking were her eyes; not just for their color, which was a remarkable green dotted with flecks of brown and gray, but also for their size: though lovely, they seemed, in relation to the rest of her features, almost too large for her face. And they looked at you with a keen, searching sort of intensity, like the eyes of nocturnal animals—discerning, compelling, demanding one's attention. Sarah was attractive. Even, in a well-scrubbed, all-American, T-shirt-and-jeans sort of way—beautiful.

Cars can be beautiful too, but I'd never keep one in Manhattan. No matter how beautiful, how magnificent. In fact, the more impressive the car, the less likely I'd be to keep it. It's not the right place, the right time, for a beautiful car. Too risky, too expensive. At that moment, my mind, my heart, were in a Manhattan-like state. It was no place for something beautiful. I didn't need the complication. Didn't want the hassle, the worry.

"You know," I said, "I'm just getting over a bout of the flu. Don't think I'm up for a dance. But thanks."

Sarah Mitchell, high school friend of the bride, gave me a small, tight-lipped grin, nodded her pretty head, and walked away.

. . .

Driving back to the city the next day, Alex scolded me.

"Why didn't you talk to her?"

"I did talk to her."

"Yeah, you told her to go away."

"No I didn't. I just said I didn't feel like dancing."

"And why'd you do that?"

"Do I have to dance with everyone who asks?"

Alex frowned. "Who else asked?"

I ignored the question. "How do you know about this anyway?"

"Everyone knows about it."

"How?"

"It wasn't a big wedding, Jack."

"It was a hundred and fifty people!"

He didn't respond.

I was quiet for a while, stewing over Alex's interrogation and the fact that my behavior had been so closely scrutinized. "I told you," I said finally, "I've given up women. At least for a while. And the last thing I need in my life is someone fishing for a husband."

"How do you know she's fishing?"

"You're the one who said that."

"I didn't say *she* was." He paused a moment. "She was hot."

I said nothing.

"And smart. Graduated from Penn. Columbia Law. Lives on the East Side. Works at a—"

"Are you her agent?" I snapped.

"Just giving you the information, dude."

"I didn't ask for any information."

"Jack," he groaned, "don't write the girl off for no good reason."

This from a man who had stopped seeing a woman not long before because she had refused to accommodate his prurient request that she shave her pubic hair. Not *trim*, mind you—*shave*. "Hell, if she won't even do that for you," he had ranted at the time, "why waste your time with her, you know? What's the point?"

More than horrified, I was confused. "But isn't that kind of a *personal* thing?" I'd said, trying not to betray too much sarcasm. "I mean, aside from why you would even *ask* . . ."— I couldn't imagine—". . . why is it so important, so wrong, that she said no?"

"Because it's a simple request!" he'd answered indignantly. "And it's something that's easy to do. It only takes a few minutes, and no one else will know she did it—just me. I mean, for chrissake, if she won't meet you halfway on something so easy, what's next?"

It had bothered me profoundly that such a position should have any kind of logical basis.

And so, back in the car, I simply said to him, "Look, if you like Sarah so damn much, why don't you ask her out?"

"Not my type," he said. "She's your type. And besides, word is she liked you."

"She doesn't even know me. We talked for three minutes. And, according to you, I insulted her."

He gave a huff of exasperation. "When Tom and Michelle get back from their honeymoon, you should call and get her number."

After a few moments of silent frustration, I changed the subject. "Noticed you didn't make it back to the room last night."

A pause, then a debauched chuckle. "Found alternate ac-
commodations, dude."

"A certain bridesmaid? The blonde?" Looking over, I saw
the grin: wide, self-satisfied, unmistakable.

"Nice girl," he said.

Chapter 3

The following Wednesday I arrived an hour late at the birthday party for a friend. It was a small, casual affair in the
West Village apartment she shared with her boyfriend Matt,
a commodities trader at some investment fund. Still, the
twenty bodies who had arrived before me filled the living
room and this, together with the up-tempo jazz on the stereo,
gave the gathering the frantic, heady feel of a genuine bash.
Scanning the crowd just inside the door, I spotted Janie; she
hurried over.

"Jack!" she laughed, hugging my shoulders. "Thanks so
much for coming!"

"Sorry I'm late," I said, handing her the bottle of wine I'd
brought along. "Got hung up, as usual." I kissed her on the
cheek. "Happy birthday."

"Thanks, sweetie."

I glanced quickly around the room. "So this is the place."

"Yes!" she said beaming, extending her arms from her sides as if to gather it all in. "We've been here a month now. This is kind of a combination birthday and apartment-warming party." Another bright smile.

I'd always found Janie attractive: about five-seven, short dark hair, cute Italian features. We knew each other from graduate school, where we'd dated briefly but ultimately decided to "just be friends." She tugged on my arm: "Let me give you the tour."

The apartment was a large two-bedroom, beautifully appointed, with an enormous living room and a kitchen big enough for a small breakfast table. Still living in a one-room box myself, I stared with envy.

"We want to be here awhile," she said, "so we bit the bullet financially to get the extra space."

"You must have bit hard," I said.

The place was spectacular. And as the tour continued, it occurred to me that, aside from the regular and hassle-free relief of the urge to copulate, there may be no more singularly powerful incentive for human beings to couple up than the obscene cost of housing in New York City. Looking into the second bedroom, realizing that it was almost the size of my entire apartment, my repudiative policy regarding wage-earning women began to soften. At least in theory.

We came to a door. Janie opened it, poked her head in, then backed out. "Matt's on a call to Tokyo," she whispered. "That's the study. I'll show it to you later."

With the tour interrupted, Janie flitted off to attend to other guests. I returned to the living room. Maneuvering around bodies, I made my way to the bar—a random array of booze, mixers, and wine set up on a table at one end of the living room. I'd just poured myself a drink when I heard: "We have to stop meeting this way."

I spun around. It took me a moment, but then: "*Sarah?*"

"I seem to always find you at the bar." She laughed. "Typical writer."

Recovering from my surprise, I somehow managed, with all the wit and panache of a financial analyst: "Two observations don't make a trend." Sarah smiled graciously. "And besides," I continued, holding up my glass, "it's only soda."

"Do you not drink?"

"Gave it up."

"How come?"

"Alcohol is poison."

Sarah's face crinkled. "It is?"

"It is for me."

Her quizzical glance and crooked grin made clear she wanted more information, but I offered none; was too distracted. And it wasn't just the stunning randomness of our meeting again. Sarah looked different somehow. Softer. Then I realized: it was her hair. At the wedding it was tucked up behind her head. Elegant, but formal. It fell naturally now, just below her shoulders, framing her face in a gloriously feminine, almost angelic way. There was no denying it—she looked sensational.

"How're you feeling?" she asked.

"What?"

"The flu."

"Oh, right." I nodded stiffly. "Much better, thanks. So . . . what are you doing here?"

Sarah's eyes widened with mock reproach. "Same thing you are, I guess!"

"Sorry," I said, my face warming. "The surprise has got me flustered. How do you know Janie?"

"She lives with my brother."

Again my brain was blasted. I stared at Sarah. "Wait . . . Matt is your *brother*?"

She nodded, smiling.

I shook my head, as if to dislodge the cobwebs.

"You assumed I knew Janie," she said.

"Yeah," I acknowledged. "Don't really know why, now that I think about it."

"Same reason you were surprised I play guitar."

Embarrassed, I took a thoughtful sip of my soda. Looking back at her, I frowned penitently. "Strange how one's thinking can be determined by a few assumptions." I meant this as a kind of apology. Sarah seemed to take it that way.

"We're all prone to that," she said, her mouth turned up at the corner.

I held her glance for a moment; she'd let me off the hook. "So what do you think of the apartment?" I asked, moving on.

"I *love* it!" she gushed, looking about with bright, fascinated eyes. "I'm so jealous! Have you seen the whole place?"

Except for the study, I told her. "Matt . . . your brother"— I still couldn't believe the coincidence—"was on the phone when Janie was showing me around."

"Oh, you *have* to see it," Sarah said. Taking my free hand, she tugged me through and around the other guests. Moving down the hallway, we found the door open—the room no longer the site of trans-Pacific commodities dealing. "Isn't this incredible?" she said, pulling me inside.

The room was not large, maybe twelve-by-fifteen, but was still impressive: two of the walls were floor-to-ceiling bookshelves, darkly stained wood filled with scores of volumes; early-evening honey light poured through two enormous windows, lavishly curtained, in the street-side wall; a magnificent desk, apparently antique, occupied the remaining wall by the door, an impossibly thin laptop computer resting on its polished surface; and in the corner a sleek plastic box I recognized as a Bloomberg terminal blinked a yellow-orange summary of the day's bond market activity. It was a study, all right. Traditionally contemplative, impressively modern—the home office of a twenty-first-century financial executive. I seethed with envy.

"Not a bad place to write," Sarah said.

"Not bad at all."

I looked from the desk to Sarah. She looked back at me, smiling gently as we stood alone in the small, intimate room, the festive din of the party safely at the other end of the hallway. And at that moment, a switch was thrown somewhere inside me. Sarah was attractive. Intelligent. Clever. I wanted to know more. See more. I decided to ask for her number before leaving. But just then her searching glance had me off balance. Stalling for time, I looked over at the framed photographs mounted on the wall over the desk. One was a striking black-and-white of Poet's Walk in Central Park on a winter morning: a lone soul strolled along the snowy path, the bare limbs of the bordering trees arcing into a kind of contemplative cathedral overhead. "That's a nice shot," I said.

"Thanks."

"*You* took that?" I said, genuinely surprised.

Sarah nodded. "Remember the big snow in 'ninety-six?"

"Yeah."

"I went out early the first morning and shot a couple of rolls while the snow was still new." She looked at the picture, smiling again, as if recalling the beauty of the post-blizzard park. "I was coming up the hill toward the Met when I saw this person walking alone under the trees. It was so perfect. Taking the shot felt almost like stealing."

I nearly asked her to dinner right then. But still stalling, I said instead, "You've studied photography?"

She laughed. "Oh, no. Just a now-and-then hobby. I really do enjoy it, though. I wish I had more time."

I nodded, then looked again at the shot. The picture immediately adjacent showed Janie posing happily with Al Gore. I suddenly remembered that while in college she'd been an intern on the staff of Senator Daniel Patrick Moynihan.

"So what do you think about Mr. Gore?" I said, trying to make easy conversation.

Sarah seemed confused by the nature and timing of the question, but played along. "I don't know," she said, looking now at the photograph. "I think he has image problems."

"How do you mean?"

She frowned thoughtfully. "People just don't respond to him the way they did to Clinton. Especially women, I think."

I looked at her. "Their policies are practically identical, aren't they?"

"It's more of a charisma thing," she said. Then an awkward sideways grin, as if she were embarrassed. "I know I should hate Clinton for what he did to Hillary and Chelsea. As a woman. As a human being. I mean, I certainly don't approve, but . . ."

Suddenly, I was worried.

Sarah paused, as if aware of how intently I was looking at her. "He just appeals to me on some level."

"How so?" I asked, forcing a chuckle.

"Well, I support the kinds of policies he represents," she said. "That's the most important thing. But I admit it's more than that." Her aspect softened; a helpless shrug. "I just like him. He's smart and passionate and confident. . . ."

"Some would say arrogant."

She smiled, almost girlishly. "I still find him attractive."

I stared in horror.

"He's just got it," she went on. Then, with a gushing, teen-age laugh: "He's sexy!"

"You know where the bathroom is?"

A look of awkward surprise replaced Sarah's silly grin. "Uh, yeah, down the hall on the right."

Ten minutes later, I left without asking for her number— my disavowal of the female species renewed.

Chapter 4

If there was any residual doubt in my mind, any tiny crack in my resolve, it was obliterated the following afternoon.

A knock on my office door. Looking up, I saw Karen's head poking through the space between the door and the jamb.

"Got a minute?" She looked troubled.

Karen was thirty-six and single. Attractive in a slightly tattered, rakish kind of way—thin and petite, chemically altered auburn hair, dark lonely eyes. She had joined the bank around the same time I had, and over the years had taken to using me as a sounding board to work out strategies for dealing with the men in her life. And there had been many. Usually I was happy to play the part—it made for terrific voyeuristic entertainment. That morning I was less inclined, but seeing the distress in her expression, I gave an acquiescent nod.

She stepped in, closed the door behind her, sat down in the guest chair across my desk. Within five seconds she was in tears.

"What's happened?"

"Dana dumped me," she yelped pathetically.

"The real estate guy?"

She nodded, her face flushing.

I'd never liked Dana, even though I'd never met him. I instinctively dislike men with names like Dana. "I'm sorry," I lied.

"Everything was going so well," she said, wiping her nose with a tissue from my desk. "And then, boom, just like that, out of nowhere, he *dumps* me." Another quiet convulsion.

I remained silent, figuring I should just listen.

"I don't understand men," she declared bitterly. She cried some more and then, dabbing at her eyes, looked up at me as if to say, *You're supposed to say something comforting, damn it!*

I decided instead to give it to her straight. It was my cynical mood. And the fact that this was the fourth or fifth time I'd sat through this with Karen. It seemed so basic, so obvious—she couldn't possibly not *know*. She was, after all, a thirty-six-year-old woman with nearly twenty years' experience with all this. And yet apparently, astonishingly, for whatever reason, Karen was in need of reminding.

"How long was it before you slept with him?" I asked.

At this, she looked at me with shocked eyes and comically contrived innocence.

"Come off it," I said.

She dropped her glance to her lap.

"And don't lie."

She looked up, frowning. "Our second date."

I chuckled. I couldn't help it. "You lost him right there."

Her face pinched. "What?"

"It was probably over that night."

Her eyes narrowed. "But that was four months ago."

"I'm sure it was."

"But he kept calling me."

"I'm sure he did."

She studied me, a kind of sad horror darkening her face. "He said he loved me."

"Oh, for God's sake, Karen."

"But . . ."

"Men don't marry women they think are easy. You know that."

She looked up with a start, her face hard, her eyes glassy. No woman likes to think of herself as easy—no matter how easy she is. Which only proves that what I was about to re-explain to Karen is entirely logical *and* that women themselves recognize its logic on some level.

"Value is inversely proportional to availability," I said. A financial reference came to mind: "Inflation always leads to devaluation." I raised my eyebrows—*capisce*?

Karen gave me an eye-rolling nod, as if I were her dentist explaining the benefits of flossing.

"Men are territorial," I continued. "We're selfish. We want our own stuff, our own turf. And that includes women. Easy women don't appeal to our territorial nature." I stopped; looked hard at her. "You know this, right? This isn't a news flash."

"But why would he think I've been with lots of other guys?"

"Well, if you're hopping in the sack with him on the second date, that's a worrisome indicator." Then I added: "Which in this case happens to be accurate."

Again the steely glare.

I went on. "Men understand that if she does it with you, that's probably the way she operates. Not likely that it's your unique charm and charisma that inspire her behavior."

With her back against the wall, Karen went on the offensive. "Well, it's *not* as if he *fought* me off," she said, biting off her words. "He was *perfectly* willing."

"Of course he was. If you're giving it away, he'll take it. In fact, he'll try just about anything to get you into bed."

"But that doesn't make any sense!"

"It makes perfect sense. Look, what are the chances that any random bimbo he goes out with will turn out to be the one? The person he wants to marry. Slim, right? So he might as well dive in if the opportunity presents itself."

Blank expression.

"And secondly, the only way he'll really feel confident that you're in fact *not* easy, that you *haven't* been around, that you're worthy to be his wife and the mother of his adorable children, is if he tests you. Pushes you. If you give in and fail the test, then you're not the one, it doesn't matter, and he'll just indulge himself."

Stunned, she simply stared.

"Perfectly logical," I said.

She sat quietly for a few moments, then: "So you're saying I shouldn't ever sleep with anyone?"

I shook my head. "I'm not saying that at all. In fact, most men won't marry a woman they haven't slept with."

"*What?*"

"Well, that makes sense, right? You're signing a lifetime contract. Or a long one anyway. You want to make sure you're compatible."

Growing angry now: "So, if I'm really interested in a guy, I shouldn't sleep with him too soon or he'll think I'm a slut and dump me. But I *should* sleep with him at some point or he'll think I'm frigid and dump me."

"Exactly."

"So when is not too soon and not too late?"

I frowned. "Therein lies the mystery. Every guy is different."

Her eyes blazed contempt. "So I should run my sex life to satisfy the stupid, ridiculous, selfish expectations of *men?*" she scoffed, suddenly the inspired feminist.

"I'm saying you have to keep your eye on the ball. It's up to you what the ball is. If it's your desire to boff some guy, that's your decision. But if the goal is getting him to marry you, then maybe you shouldn't."

"And meanwhile men are allowed to tramp around all they want!"

"Well, it's not so much that we're *allowed,*" I said. "Most women expect men to behave that way. They think it's normal." I shrugged. "Men have higher standards."

Finally, the inevitable: "That's not fair!"

"I didn't say it's fair. Just the way it is."

I held her anxious glance a moment longer and then, pushing back in my chair, reached over my right shoulder and shoved open the window behind me. Without a word, Karen and I stood and, passing each other in my small office, switched chairs. The drill had become routine during particularly stressful counseling sessions. Karen sat down behind my desk, opened her shoulder bag, pulled out a cigarette, and lit up. She inhaled deeply, desperately, blowing the smoke out the open window.

We sat for a while, Karen quietly smoking, me just sitting there.

"Why haven't you ever set me up with one of your friends?" she asked suddenly.

"You've never seemed to need the help," I said.

Karen took a long, pensive drag. Exhaling out the window, she looked exhausted, haggard, beaten down. "I do now," she said.

· · ·

Arriving home that evening, I pulled a large manila envelope from my mailbox. I was disappointed, but not surprised: the envelope, I knew, contained my latest story, returned, as usual, by the magazine to which I had submitted it.

Despite myself, I pried apart the wing clasp, opened the flap, and peeked inside. There, indeed, was my story, looking sad and pitiful, with a short typed note clipped to the front page. The note read:

Dear Mr. Lafferty:

Thank you for submitting your fine story.

While your writing shows great promise, I'm afraid we found the story linear and one-dimensional in ways that disappointed us.

Best of luck finding a place for it.

The Editors

Looking up from the page, I wondered: Could it have been "linear" and "one-dimensional" in ways that *didn't* disappoint them?

Chapter 5

Two days later, Saturday, I met Alex at the gym. He'd had a date the night before—someone he'd met on the subway, of all places. Apparently things hadn't gone quite as well as he'd hoped.

"You didn't like her?" I asked as I slid a plate onto the barbell.

"I liked *her*," he said. "She was fine. Cute and funny and sexy. Had a sweet little body on her. It was her pierced tongue I couldn't deal with."

I laughed. "She had one of those?"

He nodded, frowning. "Disgusting. I couldn't even bring myself to kiss her."

"You didn't notice it when you met her?"

"I don't think she had it in." He shuddered at the thought. "What is it with women in their twenties and this whole body-piercing thing? I mean, where'd all that come from? *We* never did that."

"They see it as self-expression."

"Self-mutilation is what it is," he declared gravely. "Like those crazies I saw on *Oprah* once. The ones so numbed by their pathetic lives they slash their arms and legs with razor blades just to feel something."

I winced, then said, "Since when do you watch *Oprah*?"

"I watch it all the time."

"Aren't you at work when it's on?"

"They replay it after the eleven o'clock news. Late-night *Oprah*. It's awesome. You should watch."

I looked at him. "You're not serious."

"I'm totally serious."

"It's a women's show," I said, still not believing him.

"It's *the* women's show," he said. "Which means it's a fucking gold mine for us. It's got everything: what women are thinking, what makes them happy, what stresses them out, what goddamn *books* they're reading. What they really want from a man. What makes them horny."

"They actually talk about that?"

He nodded emphatically. "Everything you need to talk your way into the sack." A lecherous cough. "I'm telling you, dude, they really should market the late-night replay at men. Maybe rename the damn thing *The How to Get Laid Show*."

"I'll have to tune in sometime," I said, only half joking.

"You should." He paused a moment, his eyes narrowing. "What the hell were we talking about?"

"Body piercing."

"Oh, right. Truly psycho stuff," he said, shaking his head. But then: "I mean, I'm not badmouthing *all* of it. Some of it

I don't mind. Pierced ears are fine. I even sort of go for the pierced-belly-button look. That's kind of sexy. But the *lips* and the *eyebrows* and the *nose* . . . and the *tongue!* I mean, Jesus, that's *sick!* And, I swear, it seems like half the women I know have their goddamn tongues pierced!"

"You hang out downtown too much," I said.

"Maybe so. But I'm telling you, I just don't get it."

"I think it's supposed to be an oral sex thing."

"Yeah, I've heard that too," he said, his face pinching with a kind of skeptical horror. "But that is fucking *wacked*. I mean, for chrissake, call me crazy but as a general rule I try to keep sharp metal objects away from my schwanz."

"I'm with you on that," I laughed.

"I don't know," he went on. "Sure, I like younger chicks, but lately I've been thinking I need to get back to women my own age. I mean, they've got their own goddamn issues, like trying to score a husband, but at least their tongues won't set off a metal detector."

"Is Black-Eye-Throw-Up-Girl still around?"

Alex shrugged. "As far as I know. Suppose I could call her."

Years before, Alex and I had taken to referring to the women in his life by way of some distinguishing characteristic or event; so many came and went, keeping the names straight had proved difficult. Most of these identifying monikers were rather simple and straightforward: his date from the previous evening, for example, was thereafter known as "Pierced Tongue Girl." Some were more creative, like "The Prosecutrix," an assistant D.A. in Brooklyn who had a taste for light bondage—an appetite that, after some initial curiosity, Alex had found more frightening than titillating.

The woman I had just mentioned was a television producer in her early thirties. On her second date with Alex, as I recall, they had gone to dinner and then planned to take in a movie. At dinner they split two bottles of wine, which, for her, apparently, was too much: as they walked through the lobby of the movie theater afterward, the woman tottered on her two-inch heels, pitched forward and fell flat on her face. After being tugged to her feet, shaken and no doubt embarrassed, she insisted she was fine. But ten minutes into the film, with the alcohol's effect intensifying and her walloped face throbbing, the woman proceeded to hurl her half-digested dinner all over the seats in front of them. To top it all off, she awoke the following morning with a shiner so spectacular that, mortified, she called in to work desperately ill for the next five days. Hence: "Black-Eye-Throw-Up-Girl."

"I don't know," Alex said, frowning. "I think I need some fresh material. A new starting rotation. You know anyone?"

I hesitated a moment, but then, against my better judgment, decided to tell him about Karen. They were both adults, I figured. They could fend for themselves. "She works at the bank," I explained from the flat bench. "I've known her for years."

"So why am I just finding out about her?" Alex asked, looking down at me.

"No reason. Just thought you might hit it off."

"Just like that? You suddenly put us together in your head?"

"You just said you wanted to meet some women in their thirties."

"Sure, but you know I'm always open to new prospects. Why all of a sudden—"

I gave in. "She broke up with some guy recently and asked if I had any single friends, all right? You don't have to go out with her if you don't want to."

"No, no, that's *good!*" he said, suddenly thrilled. "Chicks who've just broken up are perfect. Heavy feelings of inadequacy. And sexual vengeance. Especially if they got dumped. Did he dump her?"

"I don't know, Alex," I lied, already regretting that I'd mentioned Karen. "And she's a friend of mine and, yes, a little vulnerable at the moment. So maybe this isn't such a good idea."

"No, it's a *great* idea!" he fairly brayed. "Don't worry. It'll be fine. I'll be a perfect gentleman." The grin. I gave him a weary look, then grunted through my set of bench presses. Just as I finished, he said, "You know, there really ought to be rules on what people can wear to the gym."

I sat up, shaking out my arms. "What?"

Frowning, he gave a sideways nod. I turned to see a middle-aged, overweight man working with lightweight dumbbells in the corner. The man wore black, skintight spandex that showed every roll, every detail. I turned away with a grimace. Alex shook his head. "I mean, for chrissake, I don't pay a hundred smokes a month to be disgusted."

I stood up from the bench. "So I saw Sarah."

"Who?"

"Sarah. From the wedding."

"You *did*?" Alex said, eyes wide, mouth agape. "You called her?" His boggled expression stretched into a broad, wily smile. "I *knew* you would!" he said, pointing a finger at me. "I told you it wouldn't last!"

"I didn't call her," I said. "We bumped into each other."

"Where?"

I told him about the party, about Janie and Matt, and how Sarah was Matt's sister. "You believe that? One of those small-world things."

Alex wagged his head, his face cracking another smile of wicked delight. "That's not small world, dude. That's destiny!"

I guffawed. "It's random chance."

"Oh, sure," he said, mocking me. "New York is a city of only eight million people. You're bound to bump into everyone at some point." A twisted smirk. "Tell me you at least talked to her this time."

"I talked to her," I said, sitting down on the curling bench. More curls, more girls. Not that I cared. "For quite a while, actually."

"And?"

"And what?" I began my set.

"You gonna get together?"

"Don't think so," I grunted.

"You don't think so," he repeated, mocking me again.

I shook my head, straining with the bar.

"You didn't get her number?"

"Didn't ask."

"Why the hell not?"

"What's it to you, anyway? Why do you care?"

"I just don't understand what your problem is."

"I don't have a problem."

"Yes, you clearly do," he declared.

I looked over at him.

"Dude, Sarah is a quality piece of ass," he went on. "And smart. A rare combination. The kind of action you go for. She's really something special. *And* she's interested in you. But you don't give a damn. You couldn't care less. I'm just wondering why."

I dropped the bar and stood up from the bench. "Because she's insane!"

Alex frowned. "Why is she insane?"

I assumed a prosecutor's rigid posture. "You know what she said that night?"

Alex folded his arms, raised his eyebrows in feigned interest.

"She said Bill Clinton is sexy," I said in the modulated, can-you-believe-it manner in which I might have reported that ancient ruins had been discovered on Mars. "*Bill Clinton!* Sexy! Mr. Hey-Paula-Check-Out-This-Whopper! Mr. Sure-I-Like-Ya-Monica-Just-Keep-Sucking! *Sexy!* This from a supposedly intelligent woman!"

"Jack, don't let your politics get in the way of—"

"It has nothing to do with politics!" I insisted, my voice soaring toward falsetto range. "*I'm* a Democrat! I *voted* for Clinton! I mean, I could understand if she still supported him *politically*. His policies and positions—fine. But that's *not* what she said. She said he's *sexy*. As in *personally* attractive." I shook my head in exasperation. "She says she knows she shouldn't feel that way. That as a woman, as a human being, she should hate Clinton for what he did to Hillary and Chelsea, but she just can't help it. 'He *appeals* to me on some level,'" I mimicked, putting on my best bimbo voice. "'He's just *got it.*'"

"And that surprises you?" Alex asked.

"It *horrifies* me! And infuriates me! How can any self-respecting woman find Bill Clinton even remotely attractive, let alone *sexy*? I mean, the guy is the an*tith*esis of what women say a man should be! What they *say* they want! He goes out and defiles his marriage in front of the entire world, totally humiliates his wife and daughter, and Sarah thinks he's sexy!"

Alex watched my tirade expressionless, unfazed.

"I mean, shit, *we're* the ones who catch all the grief for being ruled by our cocks," I continued. "But at least we're consistent! At least we *admit* it! But women are completely crazy! They say one thing, they scream and stamp their feet, they charge up the steps of the Capitol demanding respect and equal pay and protection from sexual harassment, and then they get all hot and gushy for a guy who treats them like receptacles! That's *insane!* They say they want a committed family man who helps with the dishes, changes diapers, and plays with the kids, but they really want John Kennedy! They say they want Al Gore, but they really want Bill Clinton!"

"Treat 'em like dirt and they stick like mud," Alex deadpanned.

"What?"

"Oh, come on," he said. "You know what I'm talking about."

In truth, I was vaguely familiar with this alleged aspect of female dynamics, but had never heard it phrased quite that way. Then, as I stood there, another, more eloquent and infamous expression of the principle suddenly came to mind. "'Every woman adores a fascist,'" I recited flatly. "'The boot in the face, the brute.'"

"Exactly," Alex said. "Nicely put, Hemingway."

"Not my words," I said absently. "Sylvia Plath."

His eyes narrowed. "Some friend of yours?"

I nodded weakly, still mulling the grim observation. "She got dumped, too."

"Really? She still available?"

I looked at him sharply. "Not your type," I said, then headed off to the rowing machine.

"Look," Alex said, following behind me, "the point is women are attracted to powerful, confident men. Sure, they want respect and equality and all that crap. But they still want a strong man. A man who's in charge."

I stopped, turned around.

"And why?" he continued. "Because deep down they want to be conquered. They want to be swept away. Taken. By force, if necessary."

I gave him a disbelieving face, turned, and headed across the floor again.

"I don't mean *raped*," he said, chasing after me. "I mean seized. Possessed. They want to be Ingrid Bergman in *Casablanca*. Scarlet O'Hara when Rhett scoops her off her feet and carries her up the staircase into the darkness. They want to be enveloped. Ravaged by a man who knows what he wants. A man in control."

I turned to face him again.

"They want fantasy and romance," he went on. "They want Bogart. Or Hemingway," he said, thinking that would reach me. "Or John Wayne. A man who doesn't take no for an answer. They want to be dragged around by the hair."

I rolled my eyes in protest.

"Dude, it's true! Remember King Kong? The ape kidnaps the blonde and carries her around, right? His precious possession. He'd *kill* to keep her. She's terrified at first, but eventually falls in love with Kong." He made a face as if the lesson were obvious, then searched mine for any sign of understanding. Finding only leery bemusement, he frowned. "All right, look, who's on the cover of all those ridiculous romance novels that women consume by the millions? It ain't Alan Alda. Or Phil 'I-can-wear-a-dress-and-still-be-a-man' Donahue. It's fucking Fabio! A twenty-first-century caveman if there ever was one!"

I shook my head. "So what are you saying? That to be a success with women you have to be a Neanderthal?"

"I'm saying you have to give them what they want. Reach them where they're at." He stopped, looked quickly over his shoulder at the obese man huffing and sweating in the corner, then back to me. "I'm saying John Wayne *never* wore spandex."

With eyes narrowed in confusion, I stared at my strange friend, this worldly philosopher, this oracle of oddisms. And as he held my appraising glance, he pursed his lips and slowly nodded his head, as if to confirm that, yes, he had indeed just revealed yet another high truth, yet another rare insight into the workings of a complex and befuddling universe.

Then, for some reason, my mind actually began to grope with his suggested image. For just a moment I tried to imagine John Wayne, leather-faced, tall in the saddle, bigger than

life—clad in tight, sleek, formfitting, terrain-revealing spandex. But I couldn't. It didn't work. The notion was ridiculous.
Laughable.

As if reading my thoughts, Alex arched his eyebrows
knowingly. "Not once."

Chapter 6

Like an avalanche or hurricane—gathering force and momentum from its own self-generating fury—once a romantic plot has been hatched against you, it seems there's no getting out of its way.

A few days after my gym discussion with Alex, I returned home to a blinking answering machine.

"*Hey* there!" came Janie's disembodied voice, light and cheery as ever. "Listen, just wanted to call and say thanks for dropping by the other night. Sorry we didn't spend more time catching up. I think we invited more people than we realized. And you ran out so quickly! Where did you go? Well, *any*way . . ."

I could hear it coming.

". . . noticed you were talking to Matt's sister. Great *gir-rrrl,*" Janie intoned, her rolling pitch playfully suggestive. "And *av*ailable."

Though alone, I couldn't help rolling my eyes.

"By the way," she went on, "are you going to the ball at the Met next week? You're still a member, right?"

Indeed I was. I'd almost forgotten.

Several years before, having arrived at a place professionally where I could afford to be more actively charitable, I thought I'd become a supporting member of several of the cultural institutions around town: the Metropolitan Museum, the Frick Collection, the New York City Ballet, the Public Library. In addition to whatever satisfaction or tax benefit one derived from the donation of five hundred dollars (only a middle rung on the sponsorship ladder, the "patron" categories requiring vastly greater sums), membership brought access to various discounts and lectures, special viewings and performances, and, most notably—at least to my mind at the time—an invitation to the annual black-tie gala. I enjoyed occasional formality and looked forward to these soirées as all too rare excuses to dress up and step out. I also enjoyed access to the daughters and nieces of corporate chieftains—wealthy women who, though generally snobbish and usually more interested in fashion than painting or books or ballet, were reliably attractive and managed to carry off at least the air of refinement. A number of such events had even yielded invitations to subsequent parties at Long Island or Connecticut estates—and, once or twice, to post-gala liaisons. I don't recall much of those encounters, except that the apartments were spectacular.

"I'll be in Chicago on business," Janie continued, "so I can't go. But Matt has to be there to represent the firm *and* . . ."— again the shameless singsongy tone—"he's leaning on Sarah to go with him. Just thought you might want to know." Another knowing giggle. "'Bye, sweetie."

• • •

On the one hand, the prospect of a grand New York party was, I had to admit, awfully appealing. It had been a long time. I hadn't been to an event at the Met or any other beneficiary of my largesse since the breakup with Kim. She had loved the galas—their pompous exclusivity, the posing and posturing, the glittering delicious charade of it all, was just her sort of thing—and afterward the association was hopelessly, unmanageably close. But, as I say, it had been a while. And it occurred to me that some vacuous conversation over exquisite hors d'oeuvres while listening to a string quartet in the Great Hall of the Metropolitan might actually do me some good.

On the other hand, Janie's blatant matchmaking was annoying. And worrying. Wading back into a scene so reminiscent of Kim would be difficult enough. I didn't need the hassle, the added pressure, of Janie-inspired expectations from Sarah Mitchell.

After mulling the dilemma for several days, I decided to risk it. From experience I knew the crowd would be in the hundreds; it would be easy to stay occupied and away from Sarah and Matt—I might not even see them. And besides, I thought, I ought to be getting something for my five hundred bucks.

• • •

The evening of the ball, a cold front had just pushed across Manhattan; a warm, sticky afternoon had been replaced by a cool, breezy evening. In the fresh, humidity-wrung Canadian air, the brightly lit Metropolitan stood out against the night sky like a shimmering jewel.

Ascending the broad front steps, I passed through the main doors and entered a scene from another era. The extent of the transformation the Great Hall undergoes for such events had always amazed me. The tremendous space only faintly resembled the grand but rather staid main lobby of a city museum, looking instead like the magnificent foyer of some European castle. Part of the change was due to the lighting, which was dimmed to an intimate glow, while selected spots threw splashes of red, green, and white onto the high walls and vaulted ceiling. A dozen or more enormous planters containing trees and shrubs of various types helped turn the wide and otherwise sterile marble floor into something of an English garden. Before one of the planters a string quartet bowed a Mozart concerto. Bars positioned at the four corners of the space provided convenient access from anywhere on the floor, and a small army of catering staff, all in black trousers and white dinner jackets, drifted through the throng, their silver trays offering a seemingly endless variety of scrumptious delights.

And, of course, there were the hundreds of guests themselves—the men in tuxedos of all styles, the women sparkling in the season's most fashionable gowns. Taking in the unbelievable scene from just inside the door, I felt my chest swell, my very soul expand, with that singular thrill peculiar to the island: *This is New York!*

From the program I'd received, I knew the evening was to follow the standard sequence: cocktails in the Hall for two hours—enough time to wander through whatever exhibits one wished to take in—followed by dinner and then dancing in the Temple of Dendur. Both spaces were wide and airy; it would be easy to monitor Sarah's whereabouts and position myself accordingly.

It was nearly thirty minutes before I finally spotted her, standing dutifully at Matt's side in a circle of five or six other people. And, once again, her appearance startled me, as it had in Janie's apartment. Her hair was up, tucked into a formal little nest behind her head, not unlike the way it had been the night I met her. And yet somehow she looked different. After a few minutes of furtive observation, I decided it was her gown, which was unlike anything I'd ever seen, even given the considerable competition all around her: a stunning satin sheath, striking cobalt, bare shoulders, plunging neck, barely-there straps. A double-stranded pearl necklace finished the look. I confess, the word "ravishing" leapt to mind.

But I was resolute. I would not go over. I had a plan for the evening and would not be deterred. The night marked my reemergence as a confident, securely single man, and the museum gala was, as Alex would say, a target-rich environment. Like an athlete returning from an injury, I needed a light workout. I needed to walk through the drills and exercises of the game I'd been away from. Stretch long-inactive muscles, warm time-stiffened joints. I needed to regain my balance, begin to get my groove back. And the best way to do that, I knew, was to aggressively mix and mingle. There were more than a hundred women in the room—most of them attractive, wealthy, and eager to connect. A veritable quarry to be mined. Sarah Mitchell would have to wait. Again, to quote Alex: You don't take sand to the beach.

At that very moment, as I stood there fortifying my resolve, Sarah suddenly turned and spotted me. She smiled cordially . . . but that was all. She didn't wave, or wave me over. She didn't cross the floor. She merely smiled, and rather crisply, then turned and looked for someone else to talk to.

To my surprise, this bothered me. I wasn't exactly sure why it bothered me, but I was sure that it did. And it bothered me more and more as time passed.

I did my best to play the game one plays at such events, especially given my agenda: I moved around the floor, smiling pleasantly, nodding at vaguely familiar faces, introducing myself, stopping to chat when I recognized someone. But I was increasingly distracted. Glancing up to monitor Sarah's whereabouts, I frequently lost my place in whatever conversation I was supposed to be part of. In fact, more than once, after scanning the crowd, I looked back to the people I was standing with to find them all staring at me expectantly; apparently I'd been addressed without even noticing.

Caught in a downward spiral of agitation, I resorted to high school tactics. Using the drifting hors d'oeuvres servers as unwitting accomplices, I repeatedly maneuvered into Sarah's line of sight and, although still at a safe distance across the floor, would briefly separate myself from the clusters of people around me. Once, I even looked around aimlessly, as if suddenly bewildered to find myself alone and unattached. Sarah must have seen me—untethered, adrift, and approachable—but made no move in my direction. She was clearly avoiding me, just as I had been avoiding her. And this bothered me. Worse, it bothered me that it bothered me.

After thinking it over, I decided that I felt bad about blowing out of Janie's party without saying good-bye properly. Sarah and I had talked for several minutes after all, and even shared something of a moment there in the study—and then I'd vanished. Maybe she was offended or put off or, at best, confused. I decided that *I* would be if I were her. I would never understand her appraisal of Bill Clinton as sexy, but then stranger things had happened—Christie Brinkley digging Billy Joel, for example. I decided it would be only decent to go over and say hello. Maybe apologize for having left so suddenly. Explain that I'd had another commitment that evening.

I excused myself from yet another conversation I'd only halfheartedly contributed to and, moving at a casual pace, looped around the edge of the throng and over to the cluster of three or four of which Sarah was now part. As I arrived she was listening to a handsome, thick-necked, ex-athlete, investment-banker type, tanning-booth bronzed and stuffed into an almost effeminately chic tuxedo, tell a story about a client who had recently bought a slightly used yacht only to have his ten-year-old daughter find several bags of cocaine under the carpet in one of the cabins. Sarah looked as if she were struggling mightily to appear interested.

"What a shock," she observed coolly.

The man belted out a haughty laugh. "I told him, 'That's what you get for being such a cheap bastard and buying a fucking *used* boat!'"

I could see that Sarah was bored but, not wanting to barge in, I simply hovered at the periphery of the group.

"So what do you do?" the man asked, his bleached teeth gleaming.

"I'm an attorney," Sarah answered with little enthusiasm.

"Oh, yeah? What kind of law do you practice?"

"Corporate litigation, I'm afraid."

"An unhappy lawyer," the man observed in a knowing tone. "Imagine that." Another ugly, self-satisfied laugh. "So, uh, what do you do when you're not working?" The question had a prurient whiff to it. But if in fact the fellow had been so bold, Sarah shut him down.

"Seems I'm always working," she said with a wan smile. "Not much time for anything else."

No mention of photography or the guitar. That pleased me. Stepping to my left, I eased a bit more into her line of sight and awaited her glance. But it didn't come. She hadn't looked directly at me, but I was certain she'd noticed me standing there. Still, she made no move to include me in the conversation or even to acknowledge my hovering presence. As the minutes passed, the awkward isolation became uncomfortable, and then excruciating. I was just about to move away when she suddenly looked over.

"Jack!" she sang, as if genuinely and pleasantly surprised. If there had been any craft to her not noticing me, any ill intent, she hid it perfectly. Her expression was bright and easy, as if she were delighted that I'd stopped by. Her would-be suitor's was just the opposite; his eyes glared with territorial claim.

"How are you?" I said. Relieved to have been rescued from social Siberia, I couldn't help a gleeful smile.

"Took you long enough."

"Sorry?"

"You heard me." Sarah held my glance, her eyebrows raised appraisingly. Seeing the sudden confusion in my expression, her green eyes sparkled. She turned back to the bronzed penguin. "It was very nice talking to you. Will you excuse me?"

He nodded somberly. "Maybe we could get together sometime."

But Sarah was already past him, far enough away that she could credibly pretend she hadn't heard his invitation. As she stepped away, she threw a swift look over her shoulder: I'd been invited to follow.

We made our way through the clusters of other guests and over to one of the bars. Sarah requested a glass of champagne. Presented with a bubbling flute, she turned and took a first sip. "So what made you change your mind?"

"About what?"

"Coming over."

I feigned confusion. "What do you mean?"

"Frankly, I'm surprised," Sarah said, not buying a word of my act. "I thought I wouldn't hear from you at all tonight."

I nodded, as if finally understanding. "You're angry about the way I left the party last week."

She looked at me askance. "Angry? Don't give yourself too much credit. But, yes, you did take off in a hurry. Thought I might have said something wrong."

I shook my head. "Not at all. But that's partly why I came over. I did leave suddenly and I wanted to explain. I had somewhere else I had to be that night. I'd only planned to stop by to wish Janie a happy birthday. When I came out of the bathroom you were talking to someone else." I had no idea if that was in fact the case and, seeing in Sarah's expression that she was replaying her recollection of that evening and to whom she had spoken and when, I quickly moved on. "Having a good time?"

The misdirection seemed to work. "Dreadful, actually," she said, frowning. "The champagne's not bad, thank God. But these things attract the most horribly boring people."

"What do you mean?" I said, turning my gaze to the crowd. "They're an above-average group. They're supporters of the Met. At least they like art."

Sarah scoffed. "No one is here for the art, Jack. This is a 'contributing member' event, not a 'patron' gala." She motioned toward the crowd. "They're all here to meet people. To hook up. That's why they're members in the first place."

I felt the sting of dead-on indictment.

"I mean, if there's any conscious selectivity going on," she continued, "it's that everyone here has a bit of money. But it's no collection of art lovers."

"Cynical thing, aren't you?"

"Want proof?" she asked briskly. "We have access to the whole museum, right? We can walk through any exhibit in the building. How many people have left this area?"

I looked around. She was right: the Great Hall was still packed and loud with the excited chatter and shrieking laughter of human flirtation; I could see only a few people on the balcony upstairs that led to the galleries.

"This might as well be any bar in New York," Sarah said.

"So why did you come?"

Her aspect suddenly tightened, as if she'd been exposed. She looked away, sipped at her champagne. "My brother needed a date," she said flatly. Then: "Why did you come?"

I shrugged. "I'm a member. Haven't been to one of these things in a while. Happened to be free. Thought I'd check out the new crop of rich bimbos looking to hook up. Maybe get lucky."

"Seen anything you like?"

"A few interesting prospects."

Sarah's mouth twisted into a tight, reluctant grin. "Mind taking a break from your hunt? Maybe actually enjoy a little of what your money is supporting?"

"Think it'll improve your mood?"

"Anything would."

"Then let's do it."

Sarah held out her half-full glass to the bartender, who topped it off with a smile and "Cheers." Refueled, she led me through the mob of hopeful revelers to the center of the Hall and the grand staircase. As we climbed, I noticed how she pinched the front of her dress between her thumb and forefinger, discreetly lifting the hem of the gown away from her feet. In her satin and pearls, a glass of champagne in one hand, the other lifting her hem, she looked nothing less than a princess. And, indeed, ascending the magnificent staircase together beneath the high vaulted ceiling, the marble walls etched with the names of major benefactors over the decades, and Tiepolo's gigantic *The Triumph of Marius* rising majestically before us at the top of the stairs, it was easy to feel, if only for a moment, that we were royalty from some distant romantic age.

Reaching the second level, I followed Sarah around to the left. We drifted south along the balcony, glancing casually at the porcelain dishes and bowls and vases from China's Qing Dynasty that lined the display case along the wall. Spotting a teapot she liked, Sarah paused to read the explanatory card.

"Don't believe it," I said. "I saw the same piece at Pottery Barn last week."

Sarah gave a dutiful half laugh.

We continued along the balcony and then, turning right, passed through several large, dimly lit rooms of Cypriot sculpture, pottery, and coins. By now I was lost, but Sarah seemed to know where she was going. There was no one else around; it seemed we had the wing to ourselves.

We approached a long hallway marked "Nineteenth Century European Painting and Sculpture" and, leaving the Cypriot section behind, jumped two thousand years through history. The very hallway itself, the Cantor Sculpture Gallery, was reflective of the era, with stately neoclassical columns and elaborately intricate molding on the walls near the ceiling. Even the lighting—a bright, clear electric glow from directly overhead—seemed to convey our sudden leap into modernity.

We continued about halfway down the hall, then Sarah turned left, stepping into the first of a series of small rooms. The paintings on the walls were Degas, nudes engaged in various aspects of their toilet and carrying oddly straightforward titles like *Woman Drying Her Arm, Woman Drying Her Foot,* and *Woman Having Her Hair Combed.*

Sarah positioned herself directly before the first of the works, folding her arms on her chest, holding the glass of cool champagne against her chin. Although her eyes were keen, her expression had eased, her lips curving into a small, easy smile, as if she were enjoying the sight of an old, trusted friend.

"You like Degas?"

Sarah nodded, her smile broadening. "I love all the Impressionist painters."

"How come?"

"I just like the whole approach to depicting the world," she said. "The soft colors. The short strokes. The fascination with light. I especially enjoy the pastels, like these. They always strike me as freer, more risky than the oils." She shook her head, as if at a loss for adequate words. "It was such an amazing period of creativity. So influential. And not just with other painters, but with musicians too."

"And writers," I said.

She turned with a start. "Writers?"

I nodded. "Hemingway said once that he tried to write the way Cézanne painted."

Sarah erupted. "Really! That's *fascinating*!" Her eyes, her mouth, her whole face seemed to sparkle. Then, suddenly, although the glow of intrigue remained, she frowned. "But wait . . . how do you *write* like someone paints? The two crafts are completely different, aren't they?"

I shrugged. "You'd think so. I'm not sure exactly what Hemingway meant by that, but there are similarities if you think about it. You mentioned the short strokes. Of course, Hemingway was famous for his short declarative sentences. For describing scenes in a stark, stripped-down style. Relating the essentials of a setting or situation in an objective, almost clinical sort of way. No flowery adornment or editorializing. Just describing things the way they are, like a reporter would. Or like an Impressionist painting."

Sarah studied me for a moment, then, smiling again, looked back to the painting. "Amazing," she said softly, as if to herself.

We moved at a slow pace down the side of the room, stopping for several minutes before each piece. Walking past painting after painting of naked women with Sarah became a bit awkward. At one point, uncomfortable, I resorted to humor. "Nineteenth-century *Playboy* magazine."

Sarah looked over at me. "You don't mean that."

"Well, it is, sort of."

Sarah frowned. "It's nothing like *Playboy*. How can you even say that?"

I swept my hand before the wall of paintings. "Perhaps you've noticed the naked women."

"But it's not about the women," she said, chuckling derisively. "It's about light and color and texture and technique. About the presentation of the subject, not the subject itself."

"Well, fine. But they're still portraits of naked women. I mean, if Degas was only interested in exploring light and colors and texture, he could have stuck to ballerinas. Or painted trees or wheat fields or beaches. He chose to paint naked women."

"And that bothers you?"

"It doesn't *bother* me. I'm just saying that Edgar and the other guys painted naked women because they liked to look at naked women. They couldn't download pictures off the Internet or buy them at the corner newsstand, so they painted them."

"Please tell me you don't really think that."

Sarah's expression had flattened; her tone was hollow. I realized then that whatever territory I'd managed to retake just minutes before was now in serious jeopardy. But, strangely, that likelihood didn't worry me. In fact, to my own surprise I was suddenly in the mood for a good joust. Maybe it was the strain of my first Met event without Kim. Or maybe that Sarah had purposefully ignored me for most of the evening. Or maybe the frustration I felt for actually caring that she had ignored me. Whatever the reason, I was feeling downright ornery and was ready to mix it up a bit. I wanted to provoke Sarah. Stir her pot. See what she was like when worked up. And besides, the position I'd staked out was not entirely without merit, however crude or sophomoric it may have sounded. I decided to stick with it—if only to amuse myself. "Of course I really think that," I said. "It's true."

"That's ridiculous!" Sarah said, her face pinching with exasperation. "They're nothing like *Playboy*."

"What's so different?"

"Many things!"

"Such as?"

"Well, first of all, the women actually look like real women. Not male fantasies of what women are supposed to look like. They're healthy, voluptuous women, not waifs with implants. They have big round rear ends, full thighs, rolls of fat around their waists, and their breasts sag. When was the last time you saw that in *Playboy*?"

"Bad argument," I said. "That happens to be what men found attractive at the time. Tastes change. If Degas were painting today, he'd paint women who looked like Cindy Crawford. Try again," I said, putting on what was meant to be a comical air of scholarly detachment.

Sarah seemed not to notice. "Well, if you *look*," she said, her tone becoming indignant, "you'll also notice that the women aren't posing. They're not looking longingly at the viewer. Or lying with their legs spread. Or on their knees with their asses in the air."

In mere seconds, we'd progressed from "rear ends" to "asses." Things were getting interesting.

"They're just doing normal, everyday things," she went on. "Bathing, drying off, combing their hair. They seem completely unaware that they're being observed. In fact, Degas said that he painted these as if he were peering through a keyhole. That the bathers were like cats licking themselves."

"Peering through a keyhole? Bathers licking themselves?" I flexed my eyebrows.

"Like *cats* licking themselves *clean,* you pervert."

I couldn't help a loud laugh.

"You'll also notice that they're not sporting expressions of orgasmic ecstasy. In fact, in most of these"—she flung her arm toward the wall—"you don't even see the women's faces. Their hair is in the way or they're looking away."

"Well, if you think about it, that's even worse," I said. "One could argue that Degas didn't view women as people. Just faceless, naked objects to be enjoyed."

"You're reaching," Sarah said, tilting her glass for a sip.

"Maybe I am. But what would be so wrong if I were right? Why does the idea that Degas might have painted naked women because he was a man and liked to look at naked women bother you? Why would that ruin whatever else the work accomplishes? I mean, don't women want men to find them sexually attractive? In fact, that's a common complaint of married women, right? That their husbands don't find them alluring anymore. They see their wives as mothers and nurturers and not as sexual playthings. And that's very frustrating to many women. They *want* to be seen as sex objects."

"They want to be seen as sexual *people,*" Sarah said, "not objects. Everyone wants to be attractive. Especially to their mate."

"So if there's nothing wrong with women being seen as sexual people, isn't it possible that Degas painted naked women because he liked to look at naked women?"

"No."

"Why not?"

"For all the reasons I've just explained!" she nearly shouted. "Are you not listening? If he were painting just to get his jollies, he wouldn't have painted the women the way he did!"

It was delicious watching her rant.

"I don't know *how* you could look at these paintings—the perspective, the settings, the way the women are depicted, what they're doing—and think that what Degas was after was some kind of Impressionistic *peep* show!"

I cocked my head. "They're still naked women."

"And that's another thing," Sarah said, jutting her finger at me. "You keep saying 'naked.' They're not *naked*. They're nude."

"Oh, come on."

"It's true. That's why these paintings are called 'nudes,' not 'nakeds.'"

I huffed. "I can't believe you're trying to weasel out of this by hiding behind semantics."

"You're the one who's being dishonest," she declared. "You know very well how important words are."

"Okay, fine. But you'll be disappointed to know that, personally, I find the word 'nude' even more titillating than 'naked.'"

"So do I."

I stared at her.

She shrugged. "I do."

Baffled, I laughed and shook my head. "This whole time you've been arguing that these pictures are strictly about art. That they have nothing to do with sex. That they're *nude* women, not naked women. And now you admit that the word 'nude' is more titillating, *sexually* titillating, than the word 'naked.'" I threw my arms in the air. "You've just destroyed your whole argument!"

Sarah had heard enough. She turned to face me, her feet planted squarely. "First of all, I'm not arguing, you are. Second, what you're arguing is so patently absurd I can't believe I'm even discussing it with you. Third, Degas never married and once rather famously remarked that women in general are ugly, so your sadly pubescent argument falls flat on its face. Fourth . . ."

"He thought women are *ugly*?"

"Fourth, while I do find the word 'nude' more titillating than the word 'naked,' it doesn't mean the titillation is blatantly sexual. Titillation can be both subtle and profound."

"Yes, of course, but—"

"There is a *world* of difference, Jack, between 'nude' and 'naked.' It's the difference between erotica and pornography. Between Mozart and Marilyn Manson. Between making love and merely mating. Between exquisite wine and the crap you get in Chinese restaurants. It's a simple matter of refinement. Of appreciating nuance and subtlety and depth. It's what separates us from the apes in Africa, and those who live in fraternity houses or work on trading floors."

I was rapt.

"And finally, Jack, I know you know exactly what I'm talking about, so stop pretending that you don't."

I had to laugh. "Oh, you *know* that I know."

"Yes, I do."

"And how do you know that?"

Sarah turned away, looking again at the paintings. Her head tilted slightly as she examined some aspect of *Woman Bathing in a Shallow Tub*.

"Because I wouldn't be here with you if I thought you didn't."

. . .

One evening a few months after Kim and I had split up, I stopped by an unusual place a few blocks from my apartment. A friend had encouraged me to check it out.

It was a café of sorts, and as a physical space it was nothing special—a long, narrow room with a small bar near the front, a dozen or so tattered sofas and chairs jammed in wherever there was room, and an equal number of flimsy, battered coffee tables. It reminded me of a fraternity house or the rec room of a suburban basement. The place sold an array of coffee-based drinks, beer and wine, cookies, cakes, and quiches—all at outrageously inflated prices. Nothing unusual for New York City.

What made the place different and worth special mention, at least in my friend's mind, given my situation, was that it was also a dating service. He said he'd tried it himself and had found it not only easy and fun, but also ingenious.

All over the place—lining the secondhand bookshelves and stacked and tottering on coffee tables, chairs, and every other flat surface available—were scores of three-ring binders labeled "Men for Women," "Women for Men," and, being a thoroughly progressive, altogether Upper West Side kind of place, also "Men for Men" and "Women for Women." Inside the binders were literally thousands of plastic-laminated single-page forms that service participants had dutifully filled out.

The forms were simple, with such revealing queries as: sex, age, occupation, education, favorite vacation spot, favorite time of day, musical preferences, biggest turn-on, biggest turn-off, typical weekend plans, and self-description. Everything one needed to know, apparently, to find a suitable mate . . . or at least a date for next Friday.

Upon further investigation I learned that to actually meet someone whose answers you liked, you had to join the service for ten dollars and fill out and submit your own form. You were then assigned an identification number, which went at the top of your form, which, in turn, went into the appropriate binder and was scanned into the café's computerized database. When you found someone you liked, you wrote down their number, took it up to the bar, and paid three dollars per request. The staff would then send an e-mail to the person you wanted to meet, alerting them that they had been requested. Within one week (that was the rule) the person would stop by the café, indicate they had been notified, give their number, be supplied with a copy of *your* form (that's why you had to join), look it over, and decide whether they wanted to meet you. If so, the café arranged the meeting with best wishes. All of this, of course, would happen in slightly revised sequence if someone happened to request your number.

My first reaction to the café was that my friend was exactly right—as a business venture it was truly ingenious. The crowded room—packed on a *Tuesday* night!—made clear that the dating service aspect was both gimmick and gold mine. Even if you didn't request anyone at three dollars per shot, even if you didn't join the service for ten dollars, the easy entertainment of looking through the binders and the tantalizing prospect of maybe meeting someone wonderful (*will they want to meet me too?*) was enough to lure in dozens of people every night and get them to buy three-dollar cups of coffee and five-dollar slices of cake.

The lesson was clear: figure out a way to harness the power of human sexuality and you've got a sure winner. Small wonder that the few Internet enterprises that actually make money—and lots of it—are porn sites.

But my visit to the dating café was also dismaying. As I sat on a lumpy, musty sofa with my beer, quietly observing other patrons as they scoured the binders of laminated forms and busily scribbled down code numbers—some alone, others in giggling groups of three or four, sitting within easy, almost ridiculous proximity to, sometimes *elbow to elbow* with, members of the opposite sex—it occurred to me that no one was spontaneously connecting. Perhaps not since Studio 54 circa 1978 had there been an assemblage of people more obviously looking to hook up—they might as well have had signs stuck to their foreheads: I'M DYING TO MEET SOME-ONE!—and yet no one dared to lean over, stick out their hand, and say "hi."

The second shock came when, admittedly curious, I began looking through the "Women for Men" binders. As I read about the favorite times of day, favorite vacation spots, and favorite drinks of dozens of faceless strangers, my attention began to focus on the answers provided in response to the "biggest turn-on" query. Only natural.

Most of what I read didn't surprise me: great eyes, nice smile, kindness, tight butt, killer abs, intelligence, great sense of humor, etc. A few answers, while not immediately obvi-ous, were at least understandable: nice nose, square jaw, strong legs, fresh breath. "Great sense of humor" was clearly the most frequently cited.

Well, okay.

But what shocked me, left me wagging my head in disbelief, was the answer cited third or, at worst, fourth most frequently—hands.

Hands?

This made about as much sense to me as elbows or knees.

Hands? Biggest turn-on?

But there it was, listed over and over and over again: "nice hands," "a great pair of hands," "strong, sexy hands," "I LOVE hands!!!"

I despaired for my male compatriots. That millions of men weren't lining up for manicures—indeed, the fact that most heterosexual men wouldn't be caught *dead* in a nail salon— was clear testament to just how little we really understood about the exotic terrain of women's libidinous susceptibilities.

· · ·

Four nights after the gala at the Met, and after much internal conflict and willful resistance, I snatched up the phone. I had two last lines of defense: whether Sarah's number would be listed when I dialed 411; whether she'd be in when I called.

It was and she was.

She seemed pleased that I had called. Despite myself, a part of me was pleased that she was pleased.

We chatted for a while. Complained about work. Remarked on our chance encounters. Marveled at the coincidence.

I suggested dinner Saturday evening.

"Dinner sounds lovely," she said.

Chapter 7

This betrayal of my solemn two-week-old pledge was punished the very next morning. And, as seems to happen with inexplicable regularity when it comes to disasters and afflictions, my punishment was meted out in a malicious sequence of three.

First of all, I was late. Distracted the night before by the anxiety of my phone call to Sarah, I'd forgotten to set my alarm. Now, finally awake and twenty minutes behind schedule, I was jumping around my tiny apartment.

I lived in a studio on the fourth floor of a five-story walk-up on Eighty-first Street, just west of Columbus Avenue. It consisted of one large room, a separate but small bathroom, and a separate but tiny kitchen. Despite its size, the apartment was a comfortable and, in some ways, even attractive little place: the high ceiling, twelve feet, seemed to open up the room and give it the feeling of being larger than it actually was; two enormous windows overlooked Eighty-first Street from the north side, providing the highly coveted southern exposure that guarantees a flood of sunlight for most of the day; and a no-longer-working fireplace with an inlay and hearth of polished black brick and a broad wooden mantel gave the room a certain coziness and even a touch of modest elegance.

There were really only two negative or disappointing aspects to the place. The less serious problem was the kitchen, which was just a narrow slot of a space at the head of the room into which a refrigerator and a small stove had been crammed, with a sink and two square feet of counter space somehow squeezed between. There was just enough room between the front edge of the appliances and the opposite wall for the refrigerator door to open about halfway, or for one person to squeeze in.

But the ridiculous dimensions of the kitchen didn't matter much because I rarely cooked. There are economies of scale to cooking, I believed, that simply aren't realized by preparing a meal for oneself. That, together with the nonmonetary costs of the time it takes to cook and clean up, not to mention the aggravation, especially after work, implied that I would be making better use of my leisure time—which has a definite and significant value—by picking up one of the many take-out options in the neighborhood rather than cooking in. For this reason, the kitchen cabinets stored only cereal and a bottle or two of tomato sauce, while the full-size refrigerator dutifully cooled six or eight Amstels, a pint carton of milk, several bottles of tomato juice (an odd favorite of mine), a half-consumed bottle of vodka, and, usually, a small white box of molding moo foo something.

The more serious problem was the sleeping situation. Like many young studio dwellers in Manhattan, I had opted for the space-saving convenience of a sofa bed rather than the box springs, frame, and mattress of a conventional bed set, which would have taken up a quarter of the apartment's floor space. Each night I would remove the cushions from the sofa and stack them in the corner, open the sofa, pull the mattress off the metal frame, then fold and return the mechanism to the base of the sofa. After some experimentation, I had determined that the combination of the thin but soft mattress on the level and firm floor more accurately simulated the feel of a real bed, and in any case was definitely superior to sleeping night after night on the notoriously bowed or sloping discomfort of a sofa bed's wire and steel-bar support mechanism. Still, despite the space-saving advantages of the sofa bed and the relative comfort of the floor, the arrangement was definitely getting old. It hadn't done wonders for my love life either.

With the exception of the bedding problem, then, the apartment was, all in all, perfectly adequate and I had lived there happily for more than three years. It was small, but in Manhattan, and especially on the Upper West Side, one got used to small. And the truth of the matter was I'd been lucky to get it. At just $900 a month, you couldn't beat the price. Similarly sized studios in the area went for anywhere from $1,400 to $2,000. The reason for this sweet discrepancy was that my building was rent-controlled—a policy phenomenon to which I was adamantly opposed because, however well intended, on the whole it only worsened the cost-of-housing problem it was meant to address. But, having stumbled into the situation, and figuring there was nothing I could personally do about the misguided policy, I had jumped at the opportunity to enjoy its benefits.

And so it was around this small, rent-controlled studio apartment that I was frantically hopping as, I confess, I did most mornings. Although I lived in a single room, I was nevertheless remarkably adept at misplacing the personal items I needed every day—my wallet, my keys, my bank ID. I shot a glance at the clock across the room: ten after eight—*shit!*—I should have been out of the apartment twenty minutes before.

As I started my overhand Windsor before the bathroom mirror, I ran through the usual drill. Okay . . . wallet . . . wallet . . . Where did I have it last? Yesterday's suit jacket? Giving the knot a last yank and tuck, I hurried over to the jacket, thrown over the back of my rocking chair, and checked the inside pocket. *Bingo!* That was easy. I slipped the wallet into the back pocket of my trousers.

Okay . . . ID . . . ID . . .

I quickly panned the room . . . looking . . . looking . . . ID . . . ID . . . IDeee . . . *there!* . . . on top of the television. I stuffed the plastic card into the breast pocket of my shirt.

All right, got everything? . . . *No!* . . . I needed keys! Keys . . . keys . . . keeeeys . . . *damn!* The keys were always the toughest to find—they were small and could be anywhere, under any of the piles of clothes and clutter.

I flew around the apartment, frantically checking the surface of each piece of furniture . . . the end tables . . . the mail table . . . the stereo . . . the dresser . . .

When the initial search failed to uncover the keys, a tide of frustration and self-reproach welled in my chest. Why didn't I learn? How many times did I have to go through this? How hard is it to put the goddamn things in the *same* place *every* time I come in the door?

I began a second, more methodical lap around the apartment. Back to the mail table, moving bills and magazines . . . the end tables, more magazines, week-old newspapers, a sweatshirt, leaves from the giant corn plant dying nearby . . . the dresser . . . the mantel top . . . *damn it!* . . . keys . . . keys . . . *keeeeys!*

Meanwhile, as I circled the apartment, my mind churned through the usual litany of household maintenance concerns: shouldn't I water the plants? Don't have time, I thought, and besides, they're not dead yet—they'll be all right for another day.

Shouldn't I put the mattress back in the couch? Don't have time, and besides, it's better for it not to be folded up all day.

Shouldn't I pick up the socks, the underwear, the running shorts, the towel from the rocking chair, the top of the dresser, the armrest of the couch, the floor? Don't have time, and besides, who's going to be here for the mess to bother them?

Shouldn't I wash or at least rinse the pile of dishes in the sink? Don't have time, and besides, fuck that.

• • •

The second affliction: the weather was miserable.

Having finally located the elusive keys—in the bathroom, on the back of the toilet—I grabbed my suit jacket and briefcase, locked the door, and hustled down the four flights of stairs. Bursting through the front door and onto the sidewalk, I was immediately smacked by a wall of thick, heavy air. At eight-twenty in the morning, the temperature outside was already pushing past eighty degrees.

But it wasn't so much the heat of summer that got to me; it was the humidity, which, at that moment, was an insufferable 90 percent. Just as the sinuses of some are ravaged by the presence of pollen in the air, an affliction I had somehow escaped, my body has always been terribly sensitive to humidity. So much so that, if asked, I could correctly guess the humidity level within a few percentage points. Nothing else wreaked such havoc with my physical comfort and so ruined my response to the world around me as the wet, clammy, sticky, oozing feeling brought on by high humidity. I couldn't concentrate, couldn't cope, and, most important, couldn't sleep. During the summer months I kept the small window air conditioner in my apartment blasting every minute I was at home. The fourteen-hour-a-day use of the energy-sucking machine tripled my electric bills, but I paid the price gladly and without hesitation for what I regarded as the single greatest quality-of-life enhancer ever invented.

On the sidewalk now, the transition from the paradise-like cool and crisp of my apartment to the thick and damp of the outside air stood me straight up. I felt suddenly nauseous. The subway stop at the corner of Eighty-first Street and Central Park West was only a hundred yards away, but at that time of year the walk was a two-minute steam bath. After just a few steps, I could already feel the filmy stickiness of humidity perspiration.

Only a few people were waiting on the downtown platform, indicating that a train had recently passed through. In spite of myself, I walked to the edge of the platform and, looking left, uptown, peered hopefully up the track and into the dark tunnel.

Black as night. No train coming.

I turned away, heaved a sigh of weary resignation, and headed down the platform to the spot where I usually waited. The air I pushed my way through was heavy and *hot*. I reached my usual spot enveloped in a suffocating seal of moist misery. I dropped my briefcase and brought my hands to my hips—to hold my arms as far from my torso as possible.

But it was no use: my body was aflame beneath my suit. Every pore seemed to be opening. Little tickles tormented me as beads of sweat sprinted from my collar and armpits down my back and sides toward my waist. Struggling to breathe the thick, damp air, I thought I might do better with gills than lungs. I stepped to the edge of the platform and peered imploringly, beseechingly, into the tunnel. Black. Nothing.

Oh, God, please . . .

I began pacing. Eight steps up the platform, turning, eight steps back. The slight breeze generated by the movement provided a modicum of relief. Eight steps up, turn, eight steps back. Others standing nearby, suffering through their own hell and using their own improvised methods to stay cool, watched suspiciously as I paced like a restless panther in a cage.

As I turned to begin my third lap, I noticed another man sitting on a bench against the wall reading the paper. He still wore his suit jacket and was sweating profusely. He dabbed at his oozing forehead with a handkerchief. Just looking at him, suffering pathetically under his shirt, tie, *and* jacket, cranked up the furnace a few more excruciating degrees. . . . *For God's sake, take your damn jacket off!*

Turning away from the agonizing sight, I paced over to the edge of the platform and again peered into the dark tunnel. Headlights! Train coming! Relief, rescue, sanctuary—on the way! *Yessss!*

The train was still thirty seconds away, but its proximity had an instant cooling effect. I could already feel the bite of cold, dry air on my glistening skin. Retrieving my briefcase, I again leaned over the edge of the platform. The headlights were larger! The train was nearly in the station! I could hear it now, rumbling through the tunnel! Steel wheels on iron tracks! Racing toward the station like the cavalry over the hill!

The train slammed into the station, making a terrible, mind-numbing racket even as it decelerated. *Yes! Yes! Yes!* It screeched to a stop, inflicting on me and the others suffering anxiously on the platform one final indignity—a vicious blast of wet, scalding exhaust from the huge compressors hanging beneath the cars. And then—*bang!*—the car doors opened and . . . *salvation!* Stepping into the car was like entering a refrigerator . . . yes, yes, oh, dear God, *yesssss!* Oh, how I loved—*loved!*—air-conditioning! Wonderful, glorious, dehumidified relief! Freeze . . . freeze . . . oh, freeze, baby, *freeeeezzze!*

I quivered as the cold air on my damp skin sent a delicious chill down my spine. Although seats were available, I insinuated myself, slipping and nudging, into my favorite spot—standing, in the center of the car, where experience had shown the heavenly blast of air-conditioning to be most concentrated. I dropped my briefcase between my feet, pulled out the A-section of the *Times*, and, straightening, gripped the overhead handrail—icy cold in my palm. I was as content as any New York subway commuter could possibly be: away from the shoving traffic by the doors; cool, crisp, clean, de-humidified air cascading over me; comfortably ensconced with my paper in the protective, ignore-everything-around-you membrane that is standard-issue equipment for all New Yorkers. Beads of sweat continued to roll down my back and sides, but I knew the agony was nearly over. By Fifty-ninth Street, I'd be fine.

And then the final phase of my punishment—the real topper, the *coup de grâce* . . .

The train had just lurched its way out of the station when I heard: "Jack?"

Looking up and to my left, I was stunned, horrified, to see Kim smiling from two bodies away. I tried to control my ex-pression; am certain I failed. "Hello, Kim," I said, and imme-diately dove for the cover of my paper.

"Excuse me," I heard her say, and with that she pushed rudely past the passengers between us, blithely ignoring their huffs of indignation. "How *are* you?" she gushed, squeez-ing in next to me.

And then it hit me: the essence of Kim. Even more than her lean, athletic figure, her darkly feminine features, or her defiant manner, all of which I had found utterly delectable, Kim's smell, the way her perfume, whatever it was, mingled with and complemented her natural scent, had always af-fected me most profoundly, physically and otherwise. Earthy and full-bodied, yet somehow elegant and refined, it seemed to announce and echo the woman herself. As she pushed in next to me, it filled my nostrils, my head, my soul—as mag-

nificent, as devastating, as deliciously sexual as I had remembered, instantly transporting me, in that magical way
that only familiar scents can, to times long past and a state of
easy, gliding ecstasy I hadn't known since. As the train
bucked and rolled, I suddenly felt faint, weirdly undermined.
My head clouded. The world around me seemed to slowly
churn. And there was no escape. My favored position in the
center of the crowded car had become my prison. Tightening
my grip on the handrail, I struggled to collect myself.

"Why are you on the B train?" I managed. Kim's apartment was on Riverside Drive, four avenues west, near the 2
and 3 trains.

"I had to run an errand on Columbus," she said.

Or maybe leave from someone's apartment, I thought bitterly. In any case, resigned to my predicament, I resolved to
be civil, if hardly enthusiastic. "I'm fine," I said, answering
her original question. "You?"

"Okay, I guess." This was delivered as an airy sigh, coupled for good effect with a sad little frown. An expectant
frown, I knew—a lob into my side of the court. I wasn't
about to give game. I nodded, went back to my newspaper.

On a dime, she changed tack. "It's so good to see you," she
said cheerily.

"Wish I could say the same." I couldn't help it.

Another quiet sigh, this one penitent, pitiful. I felt her
lean toward me. "Look, Jack, I'm sorry. I'm really, really sorry
about what happened."

"So am I."

"It was stupid."

"I agree."

"And incredibly selfish."

"Yes, it was."

"I felt boxed in."

"Give me a break, Kim."

She paused, and then: "You loved me too much, Jack."

My first reaction was confusion. My ears had registered the remark, but my critical mind couldn't or wouldn't believe what I'd just heard. The statement was outrageous, colossally arrogant, even for Kim. Surely I'd misunderstood. But looking up from my paper, I was met by her steady, unflinching gaze. She'd said it, all right. And apparently believed it. My confusion became astonishment. For several moments, I simply stared, unable to speak. Her shamelessness was awe-inspiring.

"I loved you too *much*?" I said, scarcely able to repeat the charge.

She nodded slowly, resolutely.

"So it's *my* fault?" I said, my awakening anger helping me find my tongue. "*My* fault that *you* slept with a client three weeks before our wedding?"

Kim's face tightened; her eyes darted nervously about, checking, I knew, whether anyone had overheard my comment. I huffed, shook my head, went back to my paper.

"I felt suffocated, okay?" she said, leaning into me again. "Russell was just a stupid, impulsive grope at freedom and independence."

"Save it, Kim."

"I was unhappy," she went on, undeterred. "I needed space."

"Well, you must be ecstatic now. You have all the space in the world."

"I'm not ecstatic," she said. "Not even remotely. In fact, I'm miserable."

"Sorry to hear that."

"I miss you, Jack."

I guffawed.

"Could we get together?"

Again I was flabbergasted. Again I stared. Again her gaze was unflinching, insistent, shameless. "Are you completely insane?" I asked, and quite seriously.

"I was," she said. "But I'm not anymore." Then, as if on cue, her unyielding eyes softened, displaying for my consideration the merest hint of girlish vulnerability. "Couldn't we just get together?" she pleaded.

I studied her another moment, then, utterly boggled, looked away. As I did, I noticed a large black woman sitting on the bench immediately before me and looking directly into my eyes. It was clear from her flat, deliberately vacant expression that she'd been following every word of the conversation. I was taken aback. Despite our ridiculous subway car proximity—how could she *not* have overheard?—I felt violated, a victim of eavesdropping. I stared back at her with indignant reproach. But to my amazement, the woman did not avert her glance. Instead, certain now that she had my attention, she closed her eyes and slowly, almost imperceptibly, shook her head back and forth: *Don't do it!*

Astonished, I stared at the woman a moment longer, then cut my eyes away . . . thinking, puzzling.

The forward heave of the train as it howled into the next station jolted me from my trance. The car doors flew open. I looked up—Rockefeller Center, my stop. Turning quickly to Kim, I shook my head. "Sorry," I said.

With that, I shoved my way out of the car.

. . .

My phone was ringing as I pushed open the door to my office. Tossing my briefcase in the corner, I leaned over the desk and snatched up the receiver.

"Would you *please* reconsider?"

My capacity for shock and outrage had been exhausted. By now, I was merely numb. "Kim . . ."

"Look," she interrupted pleadingly, "I know I have no right, but . . . Jack, I can only apologize so many times. Do you want to hear it again? Okay, I'm sorry, sorry, so terribly, *terribly* sorry." This was followed by something that sounded like a small yelp of anguish. Or merely frustration at having to work so hard to get her way. "Jack, I'm a human being. I'm not perfect and never claimed to be. I know I hurt you, but you *can't* be so cruel as to demand absolute perfection of me."

Suddenly profoundly fatigued, I dropped into my chair.

"I've been meaning to call for a long time," she went on, "but I've been afraid. You can understand that. But when I saw you on the train today . . ."

Another indecipherable emotive noise.

"After everything that's happened, Jack, after everything we've been to each other, can't we just sit down somewhere? Have a drink? Talk?"

Chapter 8

"So what do you do for fun?" Those were her first words to me.

A friend and I were having a drink in the bar of a popular restaurant on Fifteenth Street, near Gramercy Park. As I was talking, my friend had suddenly looked over my shoulder, smiled broadly, and laughed. *"Heeeeeeey!"*

Standing from his stool, he approached three people emerging from the restaurant area, shaking hands warmly with the man and kissing one of the women, the man's wife, on the cheek. Kim was the third, a college friend of the woman, as it turned out. Neither I nor my companion had ever seen her before. In other words, our meeting was entirely random, happenstance—a bolt from the blue that would change my life forever.

To say that I was taken with Kim would be like saying Everest is quite a hill. She was tall and sleek, with rich chocolate-brown hair parted boyishly on the side and falling soft and shimmering behind her bare shoulders—looking positively smashing in her cool, slim black evening dress and pearls. Her eyes were dark and ardent, her mouth broad and generous. These features, together with her olive complexion, struck me as French or possibly Greek, although, as I learned later, were merely Italian. As she glided to a stop, just behind her friends, she seemed to strike a pose: her weight shifting to one foot; the soft, downward flow of her black dress breaking over an artfully bowed hip; one willowy arm tucked shyly, or slyly, behind her back, the other hanging at her side; a fashionably minuscule handbag dangling from the gold chain clenched in her fist. This arrangement of herself, though casually patient and no doubt comfortable, also seemed to convey, at least to my devouring eye, a tantalizing combination of feminine propriety and sexual confidence.

And, indeed, for all her shimmering elegance, there was something strikingly earthy about Kim, something hungry. It was her full, sensuous lips, her dark features. The way her avid eyes slowly swept the area. In a word, Kim was stunning—a genuine, grade-A head-spinner. The kind of woman you simply can't help looking at, no matter how much trouble it gets you in.

Introductions were made; Kim shook my hand without comment.

As the tag-alongs, she and I stood by quietly while our friends happily gabbed. The moments passed and the situation became increasingly awkward. As I bounced nervously on the balls of my feet, hands jammed into my pockets, trying not to stare too obviously, Kim cut quick, expectant looks from our friends to me, her lips curling into a silly, self-amused little grin, aware, as she was, that I was desperately trying to think of something clever to say. Once or twice her dark, glistening eyes would linger on me, run the length of me, head to foot, sizing me up, it seemed, like a famished lioness eyeing her targeted kill. Months later she confessed that she was trying to imagine me naked. If I had known that at the time, or even suspected it, I surely would have hyperventilated. Or worse. But even not knowing, her blatantly appraising gaze had me utterly unnerved. My mind was a total blank.

Finally, with the moments passing, the situation almost painfully ridiculous, I stepped forward and blurted, "Do you live in the city?"

Kim nodded. Then her lips puckered again, her little grin tighter this time, more condescending than knowing, a smirk really, one that seemed to say that she found my attempt at clever conversation pathetically inadequate.

Then, as I sustained the impact of that grin, she suddenly leaned toward me and, with her face only inches from mine, her rich, bewildering scent enveloping me, said: "So what do you do for fun?" The voice was low yet full-bodied, like a moan of wind, and at its sound I shuddered slightly, as if at the first swallow of cold scotch.

Her question confused me. It was strange—a non sequitur. Rather than the standard perfunctory remark, like, "So what do you do?" or "How do you know so-and-so?" Kim's question was oddly personal, even intimate, as though she had no patience for mindless pleasantries. I opened my mouth to respond, then froze. With a start that left me momentarily incapacitated, I realized that Kim's question was loaded—a rhetorical shotgun stuck right in my face. Though casually asked and seemingly innocent, the question was, in fact, deliberate and calculated. A double entendre, with triple-packed sexual punch. The kind of thing Lauren Bacall would say, like: "Just put your lips together . . . and blow."

It was, I realized to my horror, a test, meant to rock me back on my heels and determine, in mere seconds, just who I was and what I was made of. As Kim calmly awaited my response, cat-like curiosity etched in her magnificent features, it occurred to me that I was way, *way* out of my league.

If I were more clever, more collected, more self-possessed—if I were Bogie—I might have held Kim's penetrating gaze and responded with something equally challenging, something like: "Spend an evening with me, gorgeous, and find out for yourself," or maybe even, "I like to tie beautiful women to my bed and lick every square inch of their body." But sadly, such command, such cool spontaneity, is beyond my capacity. Instead, I coughed nervously, shrugged awkwardly, and said, "Well, I like movies. And music. *Live* music," I added, hoping to seem hip and thoroughly in the know. "I go downtown sometimes to the jazz and blues clubs." I punctuated this by nodding my head, pursing my lips self-assuredly.

Kim's smoldering eyes frosted over. They seemed to say, "You had your shot, you blew it, I have no more time for you." She gave a small, dismissive smile, and then, stepping to her right, rejoined the conversation of the others. I stood there for three or four interminable minutes feeling outmatched, outclassed, and like a complete loser.

Out on the sidewalk, my friend asked, "So what did she say to you?"

"Nothing, really," I said, disgusted with myself.

The next day, my phone rang at work. It was Kim. "I enjoyed meeting you last night." I was bowled over. We met for dinner the next evening.

Months later, after we'd begun dating, I asked Kim why she had called after my dreadful performance.

She'd laughed. "You were so cute trying hard to be cool."

Apparently, miraculously, my utter inability to play the game, to deliver the line, had struck her as genuine and refreshing. By failing her test, it seems, I'd passed.

Most of our friends thought we were crazy and gave us long-shot odds at best. Even Alex, rarely a source of reasoned judgment, discounted our chances. "Don't get me wrong, dude," he said, "the chick is gorgeous. Play that hand as long as you can." Then, shaking his head and frowning thoughtfully: "But long term, I don't see a whole lot in common here."

And he was right. In many ways Kim and I were perfect opposites. She was carefree and spontaneous; I was deliberate. She was stylish and sophisticated, and could work a room with Clintonesque aplomb; I was quiet and reserved. An event planner by profession and temperament, Kim was a portal into the world of scenesters and fashionistas—a world I knew existed but had never dreamed I'd experience: lavish fund-raisers at the city's best hotels and museums; hassle-free entry to the VIP rooms of the most exclusive downtown clubs; paparazzi-pestered after-parties celebrating movie premieres or magazine launches. I took her to plays and Yankee games, introduced her to Roth and Styron, Sinatra and Coltrane.

But to us, that was precisely the point: we balanced each other. Kim brought fun and levity into my life, while I provided boundaries and ballast—a kind of grounding she had come to realize she needed.

And, in truth, we reveled in our undeniable oddness as a couple. Kim enjoyed corrupting "my altar boy," as she called me, and, naturally, I enjoyed with irrepressible glee the emancipating thrill of being corrupted. There were tensions and even bitter fights, but the making-up was equally passionate.

I asked Kim to marry me on Christmas Eve. She said yes, held me tight, and actually wept with joy.

But ultimately, our friends proved prescient. Kim was a free spirit, a bucking bronco who could never be happy penned in the corral of a committed relationship. Faithful exclusivity stifled the very spontaneity, the headlong lunge at life, that made her who she was and so desperately attractive to me.

Considered in that light, I suppose her betrayal was inevitable.

· · ·

Friday evening, the day after our subway encounter, we met at the Campbell Apartment—a sumptuously elegant cocktail lounge in the southwest corner of the newly renovated Grand Central Terminal, just off the West Balcony. The magnificent space was enormous yet somehow cozy, extravagant yet somehow tasteful: high oak-paneled walls reaching to a broad ceiling elaborately stenciled in a North African-looking pattern; half a dozen rectangular rugs of bright autumn colors thrown over the wide hardwood floor; and warm, enveloping couches and love seats arranged in discreetly intimate groupings. It was a place for expensive drinks and fine imported cigars. The kind of place married bankers and lawyers take their mistresses.

It was Kim's kind of place.

With us voluntarily in each other's presence for the first time in many months, the situation was uncomfortable, to say the least. Obvious, mechanical questions were followed by stiff, forced answers, which were followed by long stretches of awkward silence. We filled these excruciating gaps by sipping at our drinks; within minutes our glasses were nearly empty.

Finally, desperate to jump-start the conversation, I raised my gaze and with overdone deliberateness took in the sweep of the spectacular room. "Swanky place."

Kim looked around, a wide, self-satisfied smile lighting her face. "I love it here."

"Come here a lot?"

She nodded. "Clients like it."

I looked away, frowning.

"Jack, stop it," she said sharply. Her tone was emphatic, but in a stiff, perfunctory sort of way, as though she were merely reciting the lines of an assigned role. "The point of getting together is to try to get past all that, right? I wanted to take you to a nice place, that's all. And, *no*, I never came here with Russell." A phony glower.

"Sorry," I said wanly.

Kim's studied displeasure faded instantly. She smiled, then lifted her glass from the small table between us. "It really is good to see you."

I hesitated a moment, then lifted my glass and clinked hers. "Good to see you," I said. And I actually meant it. It had been months since I'd seen her, and no matter how badly a romantic relationship ends, the connection of former intimacy, however tenuous, however undeserved, endures. "My first drink in over three weeks," I said, looking down at the puddle at the bottom of my glass.

"Well, I'm glad you're having it," Kim said. "You look tense."

"I have been tense."

"That's no way to live," she declared. "You need to take better care of yourself. Did you know they've linked stress to a compromised immune system, cell damage, and even premature *death*?" A motherly arch of her sleekly groomed eyebrows. "It just doesn't pay to get all worked up, Jack. You need to let things go."

"I'm not good at that."

"I know you're not," she said, her tone turning soft, tender. Her head tilted pensively. "I always considered that one of the most important ways I took care of you. Calming you down." She paused. "You know, I think about you a lot, Jack. I think about us. We had a good thing. Maybe we gave up too soon."

"We didn't give up, Kim. You ruined us."

"I'm sorry." She pouted, dropping her glance. Another pause, then: "I'd give anything to have things the way they used to be."

"Impossible," I said, a little too curtly. Feeling a more rounded response was called for, I added, "After everything that's happened, it could never be the same."

Kim nodded penitently. "Well, then maybe we could have something different. Something just as good, just as wonderful. Only different."

I looked at her across the table. I couldn't believe what I was hearing. For a moment I was sure she was mocking me. But the soft sincerity in her expression seemed genuine. I was still studying her when our waitress reappeared.

"Can I get you another drink?"

I shook my head. "No, thanks."

"Jack . . ." Kim's tone was gently plaintive, like a little girl, her dark eyes wide and hopeful. But somewhere in her expression—maybe the curious curve of her mouth, the expectant set to her jaw—I saw something familiar and unmistakable. "We just got here," she said quietly.

I lingered in her pleading gaze a moment longer. Then, looking back to our hovering waitress, I nodded. "Another round."

. . .

The last thing I remember was pressing hard against Kim in the hallway of her building as she rummaged her handbag for her keys. I seem to recall that by the time she managed to get the correct key into the lock, my hands were already in her blouse.

When I left the next morning, I discovered to my horror that we had left the door wide open all night.

Chapter 9

The screaming buzzer across the room split my head.

Sprawled on my sofa, I squeezed my palms to my temples and curled into a forlorn, defensive ball. But just as the shot of pain began to subside, the buzzer screamed again. Groaning to my feet, I lurched across the floor, catching myself on the opposite wall. I pressed the intercom button. "Who is it?" I croaked.

"Let me up!" came Alex's voice, shrill and metallic, as if from the bottom of a can. With a whimper of hopeless protest, I leaned on the buzzer, threw the deadbolt, then staggered back to the sofa and collapsed.

Seconds later, Alex was in the room, dressed in sweats, carrying a basketball. "Why aren't you ready?" he demanded. The door slammed behind him, nearly shattering my brain.

"Ready for what?" I managed after an excruciating moment.

"We're playing basketball today."

"Can't do it."

"What're you talking about?"

"I just can't."

"You have to. We've got eight guys waiting for us at the courts. C'mon, get dressed," he said, bouncing the ball on the hardwood floor.

"*Don't* . . . do that," I said, extending my right arm in a desperate appeal.

Alex looked at me. "What's the matter with you?"

I didn't respond.

"You're hung over."

Silence.

Alex chuckled sarcastically. "Well, let's see. The no-alcohol pledge lasted, what . . . three weeks? So, who were you out with?"

"Alex, go play basketball."

"What? Is it a secret who you went drinking with?" He paused a moment, and then: "You really did go gay, didn't you?"

"Kim," I said.

"What?"

"Kim," I said again. "I was out with Kim."

"*Kim?*"

"Ran into her on the subway Thursday morning," I groaned. "We met for drinks last night."

A moment of blissful silence as Alex ran my report through his brain. But then: "Wait a minute. You're still in your suit pants," he observed suspiciously. "You just got home, didn't you?"

I said nothing.

"You stayed over. . . ."

I rolled away from him.

"You *slept* with her, didn't you?"

"Alex, go away."

I heard him move closer. "I'm right, aren't I? You slept with her."

"Alex . . ."

He smacked his hands together and let out a great whoop of delight. "That's *awesome!*"

I looked over my shoulder. He was now perched on the basketball on the other side of the coffee table, leaning toward me with childlike eagerness, beaming with prurient delight. "How is it awesome?" I asked bitterly. "How is it even remotely positive? It's a complete disaster."

"It's *not* a disaster!" he declared. "I'm glad it happened. I'm ecstatic! You needed it. You've been a total bitch lately. Maybe this will take the edge off."

I rolled onto my back, draped a forearm over my eyes in a vain attempt to blot out the world.

"So, she's not seeing the human onomatopoeia anymore?" he asked.

"What?"

"Russell. That's onomatopoeia. A word that sounds like what it means."

I lifted my arm, looked over at him. "I know what onomatopoeia is, Alex. But Russell is a person's name, not a word."

"Names are words."

"Yes, Alex, but as far as I know, Russell doesn't rustle."

"Maybe we should ask Kim."

I shot a killing glare.

"Just a joke, dude," he said, holding up his palms defensively. "So, she's not seeing him?"

"Apparently not."

"So you two are back together?"

"No."

"*No?*"

"No."

He sat with that for a moment. "So it was just a roll for old times' sake?"

"I don't know what it was."

"But not a reunion."

"Absolutely not."

"Hmmm," he intoned. "Well, as long as you made that clear."

"It's clear."

"You told her?"

"No, I didn't *tell* her. We didn't talk. Not that way."

"But it was clear."

"It's clear."

"Hmmm," he said again.

"Would you stop that?"

"What?"

"*Hmmm*ing."

"Well, I'm surprised," he said. "Surprised it happened. Even more surprised at your reaction to it happening."

"What do you mean?"

His face crinkled. "Dude, you've been afflicted for months. A wounded animal. Pining away pathetically. Incapable of moving on. Then suddenly, out of nowhere, you bump into

Kim, you get together for drinks, you go home together, get *naked*, and you're about as excited as if you'd just cleaned your toilet."

"An inspiring analogy, Alex," I groused.

"I'll leave the literary stuff to you, Hemingway," he said. "You get my point."

And, of course, I did get his point. I'd been getting it all morning. In the few hours before his painfully clamorous arrival, I'd been suffering the aftereffects of the evening before. And not just the alcoholic hangover, although that, too, was awful. Even more undermining, more debilitating, was my new, altogether different and wholly unexpected assessment of Kim.

It was, it had occurred to me, not unlike the incubation phase of the writing process. My habit, upon finishing a story, is to put it away for a few weeks, maybe a month. Reading it through with a fresh eye, with the new, broader perspective that comes with time away, the flaws, the inadequacies, are not only easier to see, they fairly leap off the page. Though vital to producing one's best work, the exercise can be frustrating, even depressing; to realize that something you considered wonderful and exciting and were proud of only weeks before is actually only mediocre or even crap.

And so it had been the previous evening. I was still hopelessly attracted to Kim. Physically, that is. She was beautiful, after all; still possessed the same captivating sensuality; still smelled delicious. But as we made our way through a second and then a third cocktail, other aspects of her personality, her persona, features I had delighted in—*worshiped!*—only months before began to grate on me. Her insistent energy seemed pushy and inconsiderate. Her silly, effusive manner seemed, well, silly. The worldwise, answer-for-everything swagger, something I'd always seen as a kind of au courant sophistication, came off as showy and even desperate—revealing, it seemed, not an attractive self-confidence but, in fact, something quite the opposite. The woman I'd loved for her earthy elegance, her carefree authenticity, now struck me as slick, cheap, and phony.

As the evening wore on, I felt as though I were sitting with a total stranger—and, at that, one I didn't particularly care for. The episode that followed was, I'm ashamed to say, an act of bitter frustration, a tantrum, as if I were clearing a cluttered tabletop with an angry backhanded swipe of my arm.

And yet no relief, no period of calm, followed my outburst. Beginning on my walk home the next morning, I began to suffer two seemingly inconsistent yet oddly related agonies: mourning the final death of my love for Kim, while at the same time wondering how on earth I could ever have felt the way that I had. Though opposites, or reciprocals, the two feelings did not cancel each other out; rather, they were strangely additive, at times even multiplicative, and their product was dizzying confusion and a profound, wrenching sadness. All was lost. The world was completely mad. *I* was completely mad. I wanted to die and, spectacularly hung over, felt as if I surely would.

Later, as I lay stewing in my alcohol-laced juices, I still couldn't make sense of it all. Part of my problem was that purposeful self-analysis was not an exercise to which I was prone, or even with which I felt particularly comfortable. For one thing, the undertaking had always struck me as terribly immodest, even slightly obscene—not unlike checking the toilet for blood in one's stool, something I've never been able to do, despite the impassioned pleas of television celebrities and the established benefits of early detection. More to the point, the very notion of "self-analysis" seemed to me perfectly absurd. How can one truly analyze—a task requiring unbiased detachment—while remaining the very subject of one's own analysis? In any case, pieces, tiny fragments of what would, over time, congeal into some kind of understanding were present that morning, I suppose, but were pinballing wildly around my throbbing head. Wrecked on the couch, all I knew for sure was that I felt horrible—physically and emotionally.

Alex had remained perched on the basketball, arms crossed over his jackknifed knees. We'd been quiet awhile, both of us processing, contemplating.

Finally, I slid my legs from the couch to the floor and slowly sat up. I hovered for a moment, waiting for my head and stomach to adjust to being vertical. "She wants to get back together," I said.

Alex's eyes widened. "She *said* that?"

I nodded, carefully.

"What did you say?"

"I told her she's crazy. It's ridiculous. It could never be the same."

"Was this before or after you went home with her?"

"Before," I admitted.

Alex made a knowing face.

"Look," I said, "she *says* she wants me back. What she really wants is my attention. Or forgiveness. Or . . . something."

Alex considered that for a moment, then shrugged. "Maybe she realizes she made a terrible mistake and is truly sorry." I studied him. "If that were the case," he went on, "would you want her back?"

We shared a brief glance; then I shifted my gaze from his speculative expression to the window across the room. A hard, late-morning, mind-piercing glare was slanting through the pane. "I don't think so," I heard myself say. Then, knowing what Alex was thinking: "I *shouldn't* have gone home with her." I was suddenly furious. "Damn it! Not only is *she* crazy, her insanity is contagious!" Disgusted, I shook my head, then gripped my temples in pain.

"Relax," Alex said. "You got laid, that's all. You didn't kill anybody."

"But it was with *Kim*! God, what was I thinking?"

"You think you're the first guy to ever hook up with his ex-girlfriend?" He stood, picked up the basketball, tossed it from palm to palm. "Plus you were drunk, right? So you weren't thinking. Not with your brain, anyway. And besides, it sounds like this is just what you needed to finally exorcise that bitch from your system." He bounced the ball a few times, as if pounding the very thought of her. "And anyway, who else you gonna have sex with? You haven't been on a date in six months."

"I've been on *many* dates."

"Not any real ones," he said. "If you had asked out Sarah three weeks ago, like I fucking told you to, you could've been with her last night instead. This is what you get for not listening to me. When's your date with her, anyway?"

Suddenly, unbelievably, my agony was compounded. "Oh, *God*!" I groaned, covering my face with my hands. "I completely forgot! It's tonight!"

"Perfect!"

"I have to cancel."

"Like hell you will!"

"I can't do it."

"Dude, you're going. You have to. This all happened because you haven't been out with her yet. What the hell are you afraid of?"

"I'm not afraid of anything," I insisted. "I'm sick. I'm a *wreck*. I have to cancel."

Dropping the basketball, he marched into the kitchen. I heard the refrigerator door open. He returned a moment later carrying a two-liter bottle of water, which he tossed at me. I twisted open the cap. "Not yet," he insisted, pointing his index finger at me. Then he turned and stomped back into the kitchen.

I heard the refrigerator door again, then a cabinet open; I heard pouring, then rummaging, then more pouring, then stirring. I wasn't sure what was going on, but feared the worst. Sure enough, he came around the corner with a tall glass filled with what looked like watered-down tomato juice with dirt floating in it. He held it out to me.

"What is that?" I asked warily.

"It's a Bloody Mary."

"How the hell did you make a Blood—?"

"Tomato juice, vodka, pepper, and tabasco. It's simple."

The mere thought sent an admonishing spasm through my already queasy stomach. "I don't want it."

"Take it."

"No."

"Take it!" he insisted, thrusting it at me. "You have to drink *this* first, *then* the water. You'll feel better. Trust me."

I looked up at him. "How could *more* alcohol possibly make me feel better?"

"It has to do with your body chemistry," he said with apparent confidence. I studied him. Suddenly frustrated, he frowned. "How the hell should I know how it works? I'm not a goddamn doctor. I just know it works. Now *drink,*" he said, shoving the glass into my hands.

The difference between good and bad is usually discernible, although the precise degree varies, of course, depending on the situation. As it happens, the difference between a good Bloody Mary and a bad Bloody Mary is a yawning chasm, an expanse of immeasurable, almost metaphysical proportions, and, alas, the one I'd just been handed was decidedly awful. But as it turned out, the horrid concoction may have been exactly what I needed; after only a few sips I began gulping from the water bottle in a desperate attempt to rid my mouth of the rancid taste.

"I'm going to sit here and watch you drink that entire bottle," Alex said.

"Aren't they waiting for you at the courts?" I asked feebly.

"They're waiting for *us.* But if you're not going, then I can't—they can play with eight, but not with nine." Pulling his wallet from the pocket of his sweats, he retrieved a crumpled piece of paper, then stepped over to the phone. He dialed, put the receiver to his ear. "Keep hydrating," he commanded, pointing at the bottle lying in my lap.

Frowning, I turned the bottle up and sucked down a few more mouthfuls. It flowed gloriously cool and pure through my chest.

"It's Alex," he said to whoever answered the cell phone at the courts. "Go on and play without us. No, Jack went drinking with his ex last night and ended up going home with her." I shot a savage look, which he ignored. Instead, he shared a prurient chuckle with his counterpart. "That's our boy! Anyway, he's in pretty rough shape this morning. Think I'll hang here with him for a while, all right?" Another knowing chortle, then he said good-bye and hung up.

"Thanks for being so discreet," I said.

"I did you a favor, dude."

"How's that?"

"If I'd only told him you were hung over, they'd all be pissed. The fact that you polluted yourself and fouled up their basketball plans for the sake of sex is understandable. Hell, it's practically heroic."

He tromped into the kitchen again; I heard the refrigerator open. He returned with a bottle of beer, tossed himself into my Barcalounger.

"A little early for that, don't you think?"

"I'm not the one who embalmed himself last night," he said, twisting off the cap. "Keep hydrating."

I gulped down some more water. "So what did you do?"

"Last night? Went out."

"On a date?"

He nodded.

"Who with?"

"Guess."

I sighed; thought for a moment. "Pierced-Tongue Girl?"

"Hell no."

"Black-Eye-Throw-Up?"

He shook his head.

"I give up."

"Your friend Karen."

I looked at him. "*Karen?*"

"I told you I'd take her out sometime."

I was stunned. I had no idea *sometime* was to be last night. "So?" I asked, intrigued yet apprehensive.

"It was good. Nice girl."

"You guys hit it off?"

"You might say that."

"Oh, God . . ."

His lips grinned around the mouth of the upturned bottle. He swallowed, nodded. "I liked her. She's . . ."—the familiar, unmistakable smirk—"she's a team player."

"A what?"

"A team player."

I'd been male my entire life and had never heard the expression in that context. "What are you talking about?"

"You know what I mean."

I shook my head.

"Team player," he said again, as if the meaning were obvious. "You know, she . . . goes down."

Momentary confusion quickly gave way to utter astonishment. "She goes *down*? You mean *on* you?"

Alex only grinned.

"She went down on you? Last night?"

He shrugged. "I just met her last night."

I stared at him, my astonishment evolving into a kind of prurient horror. "You went back to her place?"

"No, I dropped her off."

I was confused. "So where did this blessed event happen?"

"In the cab. On the way from the restaurant."

With a quiet sigh of resignation, I looked across the room, shaking my head: apparently Karen hadn't heard a word I said when we'd talked two weeks before—and would now forever be known as "Blowjob-Cab Girl." I looked back at Alex; his face was stretched into a broad grin; he made a *voilà* gesture with his hand. "Team player."

I studied him a moment and then, not wanting to dwell on the act itself, said, "I don't get the expression."

"Team player," he repeated. "She plays for the team."

"What team?"

"Our team. Men."

"We're the team."

He nodded, swallowing again. "You're on the team, I'm on the team. We're all on the team."

I gave a derisive chuckle.

"Look, teams share the same interests, right?" he went on. "The same goals. They work together to achieve common objectives. What affects one member affects the team. Same with men. No man is an island, right? What happens to one man happens to me. Don't you read poetry, Hemingway?"

I found this interpretation of Donne's noble words astounding. I sat with it for a while. "So, in a sense," I said finally, playing along for the moment, "Karen went down on *all* men last night."

"Exactly," Alex said, nodding. "She contributed to the shared interests of the team. In this case our interest in getting smoothies."

"So, as a member of the team," I continued, "I should be happy that my friend and colleague fellated you last night in the back of a cab."

"You should be very happy," he said, his tone, his manner, utterly devoid of sarcasm or irony.

"Then why am I not, Alex? Why am I, in fact, rather *un-*happy about it?"

He looked at me, his eyebrows tightening disapprovingly. "Don't know, dude," he said, a worried, portentous tone in his voice. "I think that's pretty selfish of you."

Chapter 10

I picked up Sarah at her building on the East Side—one of those monstrous, charmless boxes I've sworn I'll never live in. Waiting in the cavernous marbled lobby, I was buffeted by the one-two body blows of profound hangover fatigue and searing anxiety. I wasn't at all sure I was ready for this. Wasn't sure I even wanted to be. Swallowing, I realized I was still nauseous.

An elevator dinged. I turned to see Sarah emerge: black knit skirt, maroon sleeveless blouse, her hair bouncing free about her shoulders. She smiled. My return felt more like a grimace. As she approached, I noticed how wonderfully she moved: strong yet effortless; a smooth, undulating flow from leg to hip, arm to shoulder. The easy fluidity of her stride, her apparent confidence, only heightened my anxiety.

Moving stiffly, I closed the last few feet between us, then leaned forward and kissed her lightly on the cheek. As I did,

I caught the scent of wine on her breath. Nervous too, I concluded. Oddly, that made me feel a little better.

I'd made reservations at a place off Union Square. It seemed right—downtown but not too funky, romantic but not too intimate.

I let the maître d' know we'd arrived; asked him to give us some time at the bar. Sarah ordered a glass of wine. I asked for ginger ale.

Sipping our drinks, we quickly fell into the usual excruciating first-date routine. We asked questions we really didn't care about, laughed when we weren't amused, feigned emotions we didn't feel. Despite our two previous encounters, the feeling of contrivance, of self-conscious play-acting, was palpable. I hung with it as best I could: mining the conversation, forcing smiles, trying to be witty and charming. But it was laborious, exhausting work, and within minutes I felt myself collapsing.

As I watched Sarah's mouth move, responding to yet another silly, unfocused question, I scolded myself: *Relax . . . she's an intelligent, attractive woman . . . just talk and enjoy yourself . . . like you've done with her before.* But, of course, it wasn't like before. This was a *date*. A planned meeting. A staged event. A sadomasochistic pact to mutually poke and probe, scrutinize and evaluate. Regret washed over me. Feeling myself disintegrating, I interrupted Sarah midsentence and excused myself to go to the men's room.

Once inside, I cursed my reflection, slapped the sides of my head, tossed cold water on my face. The thought of carrying on with the evening was almost unbearable. My anxiety was now coupled with embarrassment, my cynicism with guilt. But living out my pathetic, angst-ridden existence in a downtown men's room was, sadly, not an option. With a final profanity, I pushed open the door and made my way back.

"Sorry," I said, reaching the bar. "Contact-lens emergency." I tried a small laugh, which came out as a cough. Seizing my glass, I shook the ice, took a quick belt, then dropped my glance to the floor, trying to pull myself together. Looking up, I found Sarah studying me across the top of her glass.

The maître d' rescued me: "Sir, your table is ready."

We were led across the enormous yet cramped main room. Dim floor-based lighting and the exclusive use of primary colors combined to produce a surreal, perception-warping mood. Bubbles of hiply obscure yet tastefully unobtrusive music—if indeed you could call it that—floated down from unseen sources. The tables we passed were crowded with people gleaming that look, that particular quality that I, from my admittedly bland Upper West Side perspective, tended to associate with "downtown": invariably young, uniformly lean and beautiful, exquisitely put together, of considerable means derived from mysterious pursuits of a vaguely creative nature, and radiating a blinding glare of impenetrable exclusivity—I don't know who these people are or what they do with their lives, but they're not bankers or lawyers or doctors or engineers. All this, together, had the effect of overwhelming the senses so that tens of millions of crackling nerves produced a sort of buzzing, all-over numbness.

Our table was against the far wall. Thin red candles, one taller than the other, stood in the center of a deep blue tablecloth, while weirdly elongated utensils that brought Dr. Seuss to mind waited beside enormous white plates. The maître d' helped Sarah into her chair, sparing me the awkward obligation. Consideration of the menu kept us busy for several minutes.

A waiter appeared and fairly exploded beside the table. "*Hello!* How *are* you!"

Fine, thanks, we indicated warily.

"Well, that's *great!* My name is *Tim* and I'll be your *server!* Is this your first visit with us?"

Yes.

"*Super!* Oh, I just *know* you're going to *love* it!"

Had a pistol been handy I would have shot him. Promiscuous use of superlatives, whether by word or inflection, tortures my ear no less than nails on a chalkboard and generally pisses me off, and Tim—*Tim!*—on top of the already precarious evening, was almost more than I could take. Annoyingly obsequious, flamboyantly gay, his affected, over-the-top enthusiasm for absolutely *everything* had, in seconds, transformed me from a grumpy, dyspeptic cad into a homicidal maniac. As he gushed his way through the simply *fabulous* specials, Sarah, clearly amused—by Tim and what must have been my obvious irritation—struggled to keep a straight face. But as soon as Tim had flitted beyond earshot, she gave up, heaving a chesty guffaw. I couldn't help a grudging chuckle myself.

Still grinning, she reached for her wine and said suddenly, "So, I'd like to hear about your writing."

"What would you like to know?"

"Lots of things. How long have you been writing?"

"About five years." I stiffened, anticipating the dreaded "So, you published yet?"

Sarah sipped at her wine, her eyebrows tightening. "Why do you do it?"

"*Why?*"

She nodded.

I was taken aback. No one had ever asked *why* I wrote and, opening my mouth to respond, I realized I had no rehearsed answer. Stalling for time, I reached for my own glass.

As I sipped, Sarah said, "Because you have to?"

I looked at her. "What do you mean?"

"I've read that writers write because they have to. As a compulsion, or some sort of therapy."

I nodded, relieved the focus had shifted from me to the motivations and psychoses of others. "Well, many do," I said. "In fact, I'd say that most really good writers do it because they have to, in some way or for whatever reason."

Sarah made a face. "What's all that about?"

I shrugged. "For some people writing is about a lot more than just telling stories. And the same is true for other artists. The work is about more than just painting pictures or composing music or turning blocks of stone into recognizable figures. Artists—the good ones, anyway—tend to be a mess. Unstable. Tormented for one reason or another, right? The act of creating is therapeutic. It's a kind of unburdening. You're making order out of a disordered, chaotic world. And that's especially true of writing, I think. Putting life on a page. Out in front of you where you can see it and analyze it. Manipulate and control it. Some people need that kind of control to deal with life. To stay sane. For some it's even a matter of life or death. Literally. It was that way for Hemingway, apparently. And Van Gogh. And Charlie Parker."

"Is it that way for you?"

"Well," I laughed. "It's certainly not a matter of life or death. Or even an act of quiet desperation. I'm hopelessly stable, I'm afraid. Maybe I'd be a better writer if I weren't."

I meant nothing in particular by this remark, but Sarah seized on it.

"Then why do it?" She was relentless, a tribute to her profession: probing from one angle, then another. It was clear that, for her anyway, this wasn't just making empty conversation—she wanted to *know*. Cornered, I quickly rummaged the attic and cellar of my mind for a suitable answer, but without time to conduct a thorough search, and wilting under the glare of Sarah's appraising gaze, I shrugged and said simply, "I like it." Fearing the curt statement wasn't sufficiently introspective, I stumbled on. "Just writing a good story, something that works, is enough for me. Even if it doesn't turn out quite the way I wanted, it's still something that wasn't there before. And I like that," I said again. "Human vanity, I guess. My little stamp on the world. Silly, huh?"

Sarah studied me, then shook her head. "No, not silly," she said. "I understand what you mean. But that's not why you do it."

I wasn't sure I'd heard correctly. "Sorry?"

"That's not why you write," she said again, resolutely, without hesitation. "I don't believe it. Not for a minute." A playful shrug.

I didn't know whether to laugh or be offended. Was this impertinence or just oddly provocative conversation? Or had she, like me, felt the strain of the evening and allowed her frustration to slip out around the edges of control? With nothing beyond her strangely knowing expression to go on, I asked, "Why don't you believe it?"

"Because you write fiction," she answered.

"So?"

"So there are lots of ways to put your little stamp on the world," she said. "And that may even be an aspect of the process you enjoy. I'd be more inclined to believe that's all there is to it if you wrote nonfiction. But you don't. You write fiction. People don't sit alone in quiet rooms writing stories just to produce something that didn't exist before. You're after something else. I'm just wondering what that is."

Tim's arrival to take our order actually came as a relief. We decided to split an order of mussels, a house specialty, followed by salmon for Sarah, stuffed chicken for me. "Oh, those are *wonderful* choices! I'll be back in *just* a few minutes with your mussels!"

As Tim scurried off, I gave a purposeful chuckle, shook my head. This was an evasion tactic, a countermeasure. And Sarah knew it—across the table, her arched eyebrows made clear that she was still waiting for an answer.

"You're not going to let me off the hook, are you?"

"Just curious," she said, grinning. "You don't have to tell me if it's private."

It *was* private, in the sense that I'd never told anyone. Then again, I'd never been asked. "You've heard the expression truth is stranger than fiction," I began.

She nodded.

"And it is, of course. Your sexy friend Mr. Clinton has certainly proved that." I couldn't help it.

Sarah dutifully feigned annoyance.

"In a strange way, though," I went on, "fiction can also be truth."

"How do you mean?"

"I mean that, if done well, fiction can speak more powerfully to a reader than stories of actual historical events. That seems counterintuitive. You'd think that factually accurate stories—real stuff that really happened to real people—would be more meaningful for us. But for whatever reason fiction has a revelatory power that nonfiction or news reporting doesn't. Theater is the same. Even though you're sitting in a room with maybe hundreds of other people, and the props are obviously artificial and the story is clearly fictional, a great play or opera will blow you away. I think that's why most written works that are considered 'great,' that survive through the ages and continue to speak to the human condition, are fiction, whether stories, novels, plays, or whatever." Speaking of revealing, I suddenly felt as if I'd locked myself out of the house in my underwear—I'd gone too far for too long. I summed up simply: "I think that's cool."

As I'd been speaking, a grin of intrigue had broken slowly over Sarah's face. Now it bloomed into a wide smile. "That *is* cool," she said.

By now I was desperate to escape the spotlight. "So, why do you play the guitar?"

"Because I liked your reaction when I told you."

"Oh, I see," I said, warming to the game. "You play because you're not supposed to. Because it's naughty."

"Exactly."

I nodded compliantly, then: "That's not the reason."

"It's not?"

I shook my head.

"Trying to get back at me?"

"Yes, but I also don't believe you."

A puckish grin. "And why's that?"

"You're dodging."

"Well, if you *must* know . . ."

"You don't have to tell me if it's private."

A smiling sort of frown. "The guitar is a wonderfully expressive, versatile instrument," she said. "It can be beautifully delicate or completely raunchy. It's perfect for whatever mood I'm in. Much more fun than the flute. Or even the piano. Plus, it's hard to lug a piano around. But, yes, I play the guitar because it's what I've decided to play. No matter what you and my mother think."

"I think it's terrific," I said in the cloying tone of the falsely accused. "In fact, I'd like to hear you play sometime."

"I'll play for you if you'll let me read one of your stories."

"Careful what you wish for."

"I only ask for what I really want," she said.

Tim reappeared carrying a large bowl heaped with steaming mussels. "Now, be *careful*," he warned, his eyes wide with silly excitement. He placed the bowl on the table between us, then smaller empty bowls before us. "They're *really* slippery!"

Slippery, indeed. The first shell that Sarah retrieved shot wildly from her too tightly prying fingers, coming precariously close to hitting the woman at the next table. Fortunately, the mussel missile hit the floor instead and bounced harmlessly under our neighbors' table, where, giggling, Sarah and I decided to leave it.

"Are you working on anything now?" she asked, carefully fingering another shell.

Back to me; I seemed unable to escape. "Actually, I finished a story about a month ago."

"Really? Has anyone read it?"

"I sent it to a magazine."

"That's so exciting!" she said, her eyes widening. "Have you heard anything?"

I nodded. "They hated it."

Her face collapsed. "How do you know?"

"They said so in the letter they sent back with the story."

"They did *not* say they hated it!"

"No, they said they found it linear and one-dimensional in ways that disappointed them."

Sarah's eyes narrowed. "Linear and one-dimensional?"

"In ways that disappointed them. That's my favorite part."

Sarah considered the odd sequence of words for a moment; then her face twisted with a kind of dark amusement. "Is there some way your story could have struck them as linear and one-dimensional, but *not* have disappointed them?"

I gave a tight-lipped grin. "Don't think so."

"So, that's like saying, 'Your story is bad . . . in ways that disappointed us.'"

"Pretty much."

Sarah held my glance for a moment, struggling, I could tell, not to laugh. On the verge of failing, she brought her hand to her mouth, but I could see the grin developing in her eyes. Then, clearly tickled by the absurdity of the magazine's statement, she began to giggle. "Your story is *awful*," she said, "in ways that disappointed us."

I reached for my glass, nodding good-naturedly.

"I'm sorry," she said, still trying to stifle her laughter. "That's so mean."

"It's all right," I said, shrugging.

"Your story *sucks*," she said suddenly, unable to resist, "in ways that disappointed us!" At this, all control left her and she laughed so hard that her face purpled, her eyes flooding with tears.

If the eyes are the windows to the soul, one's laugh is surely the front door. Sarah's was deep and uninhibited. Honest and unaffected. Mellifluous to the point of being musical. A contagious laugh, even though the humor was coming at my own expense. And as her shoulders bounced and shook, her head rolling back and forth on her bare neck, it seemed clear that she enjoyed the spasm; it wasn't just a release of comic tension, but a sort of nourishment from which she drew pleasure and vigor. Watching her laugh at me from across the table, I was completely and utterly charmed.

"I'm so sorry," she said, gasping for air.

"It's all right," I said again, and meant it. "Even I think it's funny."

"It's *hysterical*!" she said, another fit erupting within her. She raised her napkin to her leaking eyes, carefully wiping and dabbing. "You know," she said, struggling to get hold of herself, "I'd better go clean up before our dinner arrives." Still giggling, she pushed her chair back and stood. "I'll be right back." Dropping her napkin on her chair, she turned and headed toward the ladies' room.

By now, something had begun to happen. Something strange and unexpected. As I watched Sarah make her way through and around the other tables, the pretty, pleasant swell of her bottom twisting this way and that, her hands gently brushing the backs of chairs, I realized to my astonishment that I was actually enjoying myself. In spite of everything. Or maybe because of it. Sarah's surprisingly insistent questions, my surprisingly revealing answers, the slippery mussels, *Tim*, and finally my ridiculous rejection letter, had all conspired to melt the frosty stiffness of earlier. Helping tremendously was that I was feeling better physically. The hours of hydrating, the warm mussels in my stomach, and the distraction of conversation had delivered me, finally, from the grip of nausea and fatigue. In fact, the sudden feeling of normality was positively intoxicating.

More to the point, I was enjoying Sarah. She was, of course, wonderful to look at, but also smart and curious, open and engaging, clever and witty, with a sense for irony, for motive, that hinted deliciously at an appreciation of the grayer shades—a taste for the dark and the murky. She was, quite simply, enchanting. I remember thinking I would have to thank Alex for insisting that I follow through with the date.

I was thinking all of this when I suddenly heard:

"Jack?"

Turning, I looked up into the knotted, indignant face of . . .

"Kim!"

"Who is that?" she demanded.

"What are you doing here?"

"I'm having dinner with a colleague from the L.A. office," she said, her face, her posture, her manner, tense with suspicion. "I called you this afternoon to ask you to join us, but you didn't answer your phone."

I was beyond flabbergasted. I simply couldn't believe it. Of all the restaurants in New York City, I had picked the one where I'd run into Kim. "I was sleeping," I said, my head fogged, my tongue thick. "I didn't feel well. I turned the ringer off."

"Who is that?" she asked again.

I looked over at Sarah's empty chair, then back to Kim. "Her name is Sarah."

"Are you on a date?"

I coughed a mordant laugh. "It's *amazing* we're at the same restaurant." I tried to make this sound like a happy observation, as in: "What a wonderful surprise!" Doubt I succeeded.

"Jack," Kim said, her tone more sharp than curious, "are you on a date?"

"Kim, look . . ."

"I don't *believe* this!" she snapped. "After last night, you're on a *date*?"

Just then, naturally, Sarah returned to the table. "Hi," she said, smiling at Kim.

Horrified, I looked at Sarah, then back to Kim. I had only one option: "Sarah," I said, as coolly as I could manage, "this is Kim."

Kim extended her hand. "Jack's girlfriend."

"Kim!" I shot.

"I'm *sorry*?" Sarah said, her easy smile vanishing.

"His girlfriend," Kim said again.

"No, she's not," I said. Then, turning to Kim: "What are you doing?"

Her face was furious. "I'm *not* your girlfriend? We were *engaged*!"

"That's right, Kim, we *were*. But we're not anymore."

"So last night meant nothing?"

"Kim, we had a drink. It was nice to get together," I said in a flat, instructional tone, "and that's all it was."

"I'm sorry," Sarah said suddenly, her expression gentle but firm. "It's been a pleasure to meet you, but we'd like to get back to our dinner."

At that moment, I knew all was lost.

Kim turned a wicked, baleful eye on Sarah. "Oh, I'm *terribly* sorry," she said, her face flexing with sarcasm. "Am I interrupting your nice romantic evening?"

"Kim—" I tried, knowing it was hopeless.

"As a matter of fact, you are," Sarah answered.

"Well, before you get back to your meal," Kim said, her tone pure venom now, "perhaps you'd like to know where Prince Charming here spent last night."

I shot to my feet, nearly knocking over my chair. "Kim, this is ridiculous!"

She ignored me. "Wouldn't you like to know?" she said, still looking at Sarah. "I'm sure you'd find the answer of interest."

"Damn it, Kim!" I spat, grasping her upper arm.

"Go on," she hissed, shaking her arm free, her eyes locked on Sarah. "Ask him."

Sarah held Kim's killing stare, then looked at me with wide, restive eyes.

"Tell her, Jack," Kim taunted. "Where were you last night?"

Outflanked and helplessly exposed, I simply stood there looking back at her, silent and defenseless, as if before a firing squad.

"I'll tell you," Kim said, holding my desperate gaze. "He was with me."

My vision blurred. "Kim . . ." I pleaded.

"In my apartment . . ."

A high, piercing trumpet blast in my ears.

". . . in my *bed*!"

My legs went numb and my knees buckled, as if I'd sustained a hard overhand right to my jaw. Reaching out, I grasped the back of my chair and somehow managed to remain standing. I opened my mouth to deny the charge, but then realized that an obvious lie would be about the only thing that could make the already appalling situation even worse.

"Is that true, Jack?" Sarah asked, her voice weak and airy.

I looked at her, my mouth open, but unable to speak.

"Well, Jack?" Kim said, twisting the knife. "Is it true?"

I looked from Sarah's sadly knowing face to Kim's, insolent and mocking, and then, desperate to somehow escape their piercing scrutiny, turned my gaze out over the expanse of the crowded restaurant. And then suddenly, as if the horrific blunt force of the trauma around me had fractured my outer shell, I seemed to lift outside myself, my mind, my will, pushing up and out of my body. I hovered there a moment, over the table, looking down at myself and Kim and Sarah, and then, as if caught by some mysterious current, or propelled by dint of will, floated out over the tables and heads of the other patrons, blissfully unaware, happily chatting and chewing and drinking. I had drifted the length of the restaurant, made it into the bar area, and had just targeted the front door when I heard:

"*Jack!*"

In an instant I was back in my nightmare, limp beside the table, two angry women staring at me, demanding an explanation. I groped for words. Nothing came to mind.

Finally, Kim gave a last huff of disgust and with that—damage inflicted, mission accomplished—turned on her heel and walked away.

Sarah slumped into her chair and sat staring at her bowl of empty mussel shells. I sank into my chair and, not knowing what to say, afraid to look at Sarah, stared at my own bowl.

We sat that way, in silence, not looking at each other, for a long while.

Finally, Sarah cleared her throat. "Maybe we should try this another time."

"I'd like to explain," I said.

"I'd like to go home."

There was no point in resisting. What was I going to say? Yes, I slept with her, but it didn't mean anything? Or, even worse, yes, it happened, and it meant *everything*, but in a good way? A way that was clarifying and emancipating, a way that shouldn't worry or threaten you? Not only pathetic but, given the look on Sarah's face, irrelevant. It was clear that whatever progress we had made since sitting down had been obliterated. There was nothing to salvage, even if I were able to think of some remotely plausible explanation—which I wasn't. The evening was over. Ruined. I signaled for Tim.

"Oh, how *is* everything?" he gushed, flinging out his arms as if he'd just dismounted. "Didn't you just *love* the mussels?"

"I'm afraid we're leaving," I said. "If you could get the check, please."

Tim's unctuous smile collapsed. Baffled, he looked from me to Sarah, who sat hard-faced, hands in her lap, eyes downcast. Tim's head drew back, as if recoiling from a sudden, noxious odor.

"The check, Tim," I said again.

With a dark, worried expression, he scurried away.

Outside on the sidewalk I offered to see Sarah home.

She declined. "I don't want to take you out of your way."

· · ·

When I got home the light on my answering machine indicated I had a message.

I winced.

I checked my watch, wondering if Sarah had made it home and, no doubt furious, had called to assault me by phone. If not Sarah, then surely Kim. In fact, thinking about it, I was surprised I didn't have two messages. Staring at the machine's blinking light, I was reminded of an angry siren.

I avoided reality for half an hour. Got undressed. Brushed my teeth. Popped on the tube and watched twenty minutes of SportsCenter.

Finally, I couldn't stand it. Reaching over the couch for the machine, I hit the Play button.

"*Hey* there!" came Janie's cheery voice, splitting the gloom of my apartment like a match struck in a cave. "Listen, I haven't seen you in a while and just wanted to touch base. Where have you been? What's going on in your life? So did you go to the thing at the Met? Was it fun? The usual snooty crowd? Meet anyone interesting?"

Janie's scheming was not only shameless, it was laughably

disingenuous; surely Matt had told her everything about the party. In fact:

"You know, Matt told me that Sarah abandoned him for almost an hour that night. That she just walked off and disappeared. Know anything about that?" A fiendish giggle. "Call me, sweetie."

Chapter 11

I slept late in a bravely mature attempt to escape the inevitable morning-after self-loathing. Hopelessly awake by ten, I sulked over coffee.

Just after noon, it occurred to me that Janie wouldn't have left her message if she'd known I had already called, and gone out with, Sarah. As improbable as it seemed, Sarah apparently hadn't mentioned our date or called Janie looking for more information. I wondered if it were possible Janie didn't know about last night's disaster. Figuring that if she did I'd better call anyway, I reached for the phone.

Mercifully, she was in.

I asked a few leading questions, hoping to smoke her out. I'd known Janie for years and had never thought of her as particularly discreet; if she knew something about the night before, she'd spill it. But, apparently, she knew nothing.

"Let me ask you something," I said suddenly. "Do you think hands are sexy?"

"Hands?"

Her apparent confusion had me encouraged. "Yes. Men's hands. You don't find them sexy?"

"Oh," she intoned, as if suddenly understanding my question. "Well, not just *any* hands. But a pair of nice, strong hands are *very* sexy. Yes, definitely."

I tried to tactfully articulate my confusion; was unable. *"Why?"* I said simply.

"You can tell a lot about a man from his hands," she said. "Like if he's clean. If his fingernails are taken care of. If there's no dirt under them. If they're nicely trimmed and not bitten down so they're all bleedy looking—those are all good signs."

"But that's more about hygiene than about being sexy, right?"

"Clean *is* sexy, Jack. Trust me."

Well, okay.

"But it's more than just the cleanliness thing," she went on. "Big strong hands are very . . . I don't know . . . *male.* They're powerful. Capable of manly feats, like gripping heavy objects or . . . or building things."

"Building things? You want a man who builds things?"

"Well, not literally. But, yes, in a way. It's all very primal, Jack. On some basic level strong hands appeal to a woman's desire to be provided for and protected. And it's a turn-on to think of being held by strong hands. Of having them on your body. Especially if they have nice long fingers, if you know what I mean."

I knew; chose to move on. "Let me ask you something else."

"Shoot."

"Do you find Bill Clinton sexy?"

"Are these the kinds of deep questions men sit around pondering?"

"As a matter of fact, yes, they are. So? Do you find him sexy?"

"*Well,*" she said, playing along, "personally, no, he doesn't do much for me. But I know other women who think he's very sexy."

"You *do*?" I said, as astonished as I was disappointed. "Like, how many others?"

"Lots, actually."

"*Really?*"

"That surprises you?"

"Yes, it does," I said, my disapproval obvious. "Given his track record, I would think women would be repulsed."

"Well, I'm sure many are. But others aren't. I mean, it's not so mysterious."

"It's not?"

"Oh, come on," she said. "He's a very intelligent, talented, accomplished man. He's powerful, or he *was* anyway. He's famous. And, as we all know, he's very sexual."

"He's very sexual," I repeated slowly, as if by hearing her own words she'd recognize their absurdity.

"Well, he is, right?"

"Janie," I said, my righteous indignation peaking, "the man is a poon hound! A dog! A married man who accepted blowjobs from an intern!" Alex's *team player* term suddenly came to mind. "An adulterer, for chrissake! Calling him sexual is like calling Hitler irritable!"

"Well, exactly."

"And that's *sexy*? Women find that *sexy*?"

"Not all women. But some, sure."

"*Sure?*" I coughed out a guffaw. "That makes no sense at all! I mean, why would women want a man who treats them like disposable masturbation devices?"

"I didn't say women want to *date* or *marry* someone like that. I said they think he's sexy. Just because you find someone alluring sexually doesn't mean you'd want to be with him permanently. Sex and love are two different things."

She stopped, gave an awkward chuckle.

"Wait a minute," she said, "isn't that *your* line?"

• • •

McAleer's. My round-the-corner bar. Watery beer, terrible food, all the atmosphere of a neglected barn. But it also had the best big-screen television in the neighborhood, and the third game of the Yankees' series against the Red Sox was to start in thirty-five minutes. I sat alone at a table, waiting for Alex, thumbing the *Post*, peeking at the pregame show.

Suddenly, from behind me: "Where's our beers?"

He passed my left shoulder and stood before me, comfortably casual in jeans and a T-shirt, hands on his hips. Straight from work, I was still in my suit.

"By my count it's your turn," I said, still browsing the paper. "And make mine a ginger ale."

"Back on the wagon, huh?"

"I'm recommitting."

"Why torture yourself?"

"Because alcohol is poison."

Alex gave a dismissive chuckle. "Only if you overdo it," he said, backhanding the front of my paper. "Water is poison if you drink too much of it. You need balance, dude. A new approach. *Mod-er-a-tion,*" he intoned, as if suggesting a foreign, exotic concept. "Doctors say a little booze every day is even good for you. Thins the blood. Calms you down."

"Ginger ale," I said.

He huffed, then headed off to the bar. I went back to my paper.

"A pint and a ginger ale," I heard him say. Then, more softly: "How ya doin'?" I glanced over my shoulder just in time to see Alex gently shake the outstretched hands of two women seated together at the bar. "Alex Kioscro," he said, introducing himself.

One of the women looked in my direction. "Who's your friend?" I heard her say.

I turned back around, straightened my paper with a loud shake.

A few moments later, Alex again stood before me. "Dude, those chicks at the bar want us to come over." Our drinks in hand, he hovered beside the table, eyes wide with hopeful anticipation.

"I thought we came to watch the game."

"Yeah, well, one of the beauties of life is that you can watch baseball and chat up women at the same time." He leaned toward me. "The one on the left asked *specifically* about you. 'Who's your friend?' That's what she said. The pitch right over the plate." He leaned in closer. "That doesn't happen very often!" he whispered.

Hoping he'd just ditch me and head over by himself, I didn't respond.

Undeterred, he changed tack; sat down. "You realize what's going on here," he continued, his usual smirk twisted even tighter with a kind of conspiratorial pleasure. "You've been sitting over here for twenty minutes and haven't even glanced at them. That's why they want to meet you." Another furtive whisper: "They're *intrigued*!"

I looked at him across the top of the paper. He sat with our drinks in front of him, out of my reach, as if holding them hostage. And just then, oddly, I recalled my recent conversation with Janie. Glancing down, I stealthily considered Alex's hands, wrapped around our glasses. But just as quickly, I averted my eyes; aware, as I now was, just what a man's hands meant to many women, I felt the sudden hot flash of shame and impropriety—as if, caving to curiosity, I had just furtively scoped his pecker in the locker room.

"See, women are like dogs," he went on. "They smell fear. If you want it too badly, if you're afraid you'll blow it—you will. It's pussy repellent. But if you don't care, if you're beyond fear, like you are now . . . man, you are in the *zone*!" A lecherous chuckle. "I mean, dude, there's *nothing* women find more attractive, more irresistible, than a guy who doesn't give a shit."

I'd heard enough. "What're you doing?"

His smear of a grin faded. "What?"

I arched my eyebrows wearily.

"I'm not doing anyth—" He stopped, held the ridiculously disingenuous expression a moment longer but then, realizing he was busted, let it collapse. He frowned, heaving a sigh of exasperation. "I'm trying to cheer you up! Snap you out of whatever trance you're in!"

"I'm not in a trance," I declared, opening the paper again. "And I don't need cheering."

"Yes, you do."

"No, I don't."

"Yes, you do. You're obviously depressed."

I was appalled. And incensed. Lowering the paper, I drilled him with my eyes. "I am *not* depressed."

"Yes, you are."

"I am not."

"Are too."

"I am *not!*"

At this, other patrons, including the two women at the bar, turned and looked at us. I didn't care.

Alex looked around, then back to me. "Would you look at yourself?"

"I am *not* depressed," I said again. "I am merely unhappy. There's a difference."

"Which is?"

"Women and gay men get depressed. I, by contrast, am unhappy."

Alex shook his head.

"And besides, I'm fine with it," I continued. "I'm not upset that I'm unhappy. And I'm definitely *not* depressed about it. In fact, I'm rather enjoying it. I'm in the mood to be unhappy."

"Well, then it's my job to get you out of that mood."

"Why is that your job? Why can't you just leave me alone and let me enjoy being miserable?"

"Because it's not healthy."

"Sure it is."

"No, it's not."

"It is perfectly healthy and perfectly rational," I insisted, "if you have a good reason. And I have several."

"Such as?"

Duly challenged, I closed the paper and, with some ceremony, folded and dropped it on the table. Straightening in my chair, I assumed the rigidly formal posture of a news anchor. "The woman I was going to marry," I began, "have children, and build a life with turned out to be a total stranger. Not at all who I thought I knew and had fallen in love with. Three weeks before our wedding, she slept with, had *sex* with, a client she'd met two days before. That is an *excellent* reason to be unhappy."

Alex frowned, as if bored by the tired old story.

"If that weren't enough," I went on, "against my better judgment, and at *your* insistence, I took Sarah to dinner Saturday night. Despite the fact that there are no fewer than two *thousand* restaurants in New York—I checked the number in *Zagat's* this morning—Kim shows up, amazingly, at the very same restaurant, spots me with Sarah, and, somehow offended, approaches our table and announces that I'd spent the previous evening naked in her bed. Sarah, rather disaffected by this bit of unexpected news, ends the date, refuses to let me see her home, and no doubt has written me off as a worthless, no-good scumbag. The evidence, Alex, is clear and overwhelming. I am, at least at present, and until further notice, *cursed* when it comes to women! I should have stuck to my pledge of swearing off them!"

Alex, his expression drawn and sad, shook his head slowly. "You can lead a horse to water, but that doesn't make it a fish."

I had absolutely no idea what that was supposed to mean.

He shifted forward in his chair. "Look, I just think you'd be a lot happier being happy than you think you are being unhappy."

I could only stare.

"You need to pull out of this," he continued. "You need to brush yourself off and get back on the horse."

I was defiant. "Do I?"

"Yes," he declared, "you do." He held my glower for a moment, certain and unyielding, then softened with a forgiving frown. "Okay, sure, what happened with Kim and Sarah pisses you off and is sad, et cetera, et cetera. Fine. But life goes on. Time to make lemonade out of lemons. The world still revolves. And you're another day closer to the grave, my friend. So *carpe diem*, man! Seize the carp!"

"Seize the day," I said.

"What?"

"Seize the *day*," I said again. "It's Latin. *Diem* means *day*, *carpe* means *seize*, not carp, you *id*—" I stopped myself, swallowed a throatful of impatience and frustration. "You seize the day," I continued quietly, carefully, "not a bloody fish."

Alex blinked, his eyes narrowing; then he shook his head dismissively. "Whatever, dude. The point is, like I was saying, you're in the zone. And that doesn't happen very often." He sat back, looked around wildly, grinning crazily, as if opportunity were dancing all around us. "Take advantage of it! Go forth and meet women!"

"I don't want to meet any women," I said resolutely.

"That's *exactly* why you should!"

I sat there a moment, studying my strange friend across the table. Then, calmly, deliberately, as if I'd been struck by a revelation: "You said I'm in the zone because I'm *not* looking. Because I *don't* want it, right?"

"Yes, *yes!*" he said, smacking the table and nodding his head dramatically.

"So if I *try* to meet women . . . if I *want* to"—I paused, giving him time to catch up—"I won't *be* in the zone anymore, will I?"

Alex opened his mouth to enthusiastically agree once more, but then, suddenly confused, he stopped. He looked away a moment, processing my logic, then looked back at me, his face puckered with exasperation. *"Damn it!"*

. . .

As I walked home, the unhappiness I'd claimed to be in the mood for, and even enjoying, soured from a kind of seething defiance to a feeling of rather desperate isolation. As couples passed me on the sidewalk, arm in arm, nuzzling and giggling affectionately, I began to feel broken or deficient, lacking in some basic equipment or understanding. What should have been the most elementary, the most natural of all human experiences—boy and girl meet, fall in love, and proceed through life together—had, for whatever reason, become as fraught with complexity, as painfully inscrutable as any dilemma I had ever wrestled with. I seemed unable to tap into the primordial appeal, the propagative imperative, of the male-female arrangement—or to put even its most basic elements into any kind of recognizable or negotiable order. I felt as though I were marooned on some biological Pitcairn Island, cut off from the rest of sexually functional civilization.

In my darkening despair I couldn't help but wonder: Why had such tragedy befallen me? What calamitous wrongs could I possibly have committed to deserve such Job-like misfortune? I wasn't a perfect man—far from it—but was confident, certain even, that I hadn't justly earned such agony.

Indeed, was this punishment at all? I wondered. Or was it farce—of the grotesque and menacing sort? Was it possible that the trauma of Kim's stunning betrayal had plunged me into the grip of some perception-warping vortex? Some Bermuda Triangle of love and relationships? Had reality— my reality!—somehow transmogrified, been tugged inside out, leaving me trapped in some surreal, bewildering realm worthy of Kafka or Carroll or Swift? Or was I just crazy? Had I finally, after a long and bitter struggle, simply taken leave of my faculties?

Or was my predicament infinitely more grave? Was this only reality and I, sadly, only human?

Chapter 12

The message I found taped to my office door read: *Ted O'Connell in town. Tonight only. Coyote at 8?*

I laughed. I hadn't seen Ted in a long while. Not since he and Carrie moved to Japan more than two years before. We'd e-mailed back and forth, but the chance to actually sit down together, especially at the Coyote, was a welcome surprise.

I knew Ted from graduate school, where I'd suffered through an MBA and Ted studied journalism. Both bitten by the writing bug and infected, as most young writers are, with a craving for gritty authenticity (or at least what we regarded as such), Ted and I would hit the Coyote when we needed a break from the pretentious, full-of-shit crowd that hung out in the bars around Columbia.

But after graduation we somehow outgrew the place. We found ourselves meeting more often in trendy uptown bars, talking about our jobs and the Hamptons rather than about politics and our favorite writers. I couldn't remember the last time I'd been to the Coyote and, dropping Ted's message on the pile of paper in the middle of my desk, I smiled at the thought of sitting in one of its wooden booths, sipping beer in dark smoky air with the mournful twang of a Hank Williams tune drawling in the background.

• • •

Standing on the sidewalk outside the Coyote's worn wooden doors, Ted looked exactly the same: a drab brown jacket thrown over an equally drab green sweater, baggy jeans, high-top sneakers, standing slump-shouldered and reading a magazine as he waited. It was as if I'd seen him just the week before. We hugged each other and laughed about being at the Coyote again.

The Coyote is in the East Village, across First Avenue from where the Village Idiot used to be. Its proper name is The Coyote Ugly Saloon, but most people call it the Coyote Ugly. People who go there a lot just call it the Coyote. There never was much to it—just an old dive on the street level of a sagging tenement between East Ninth and Tenth Streets. What made it a phenomenon was the scene inside.

The room itself was long and narrow with a dark beer-soaked bar running down the left wall and six or eight wooden booths arranged along the right. Above the broad, cloudy mirror that hung behind the bar was a smoke-stained skull and crossbones and a sign that read: DON'T JUST GET DRUNK—GET UGLY. The clientele, if you could call them that, was a mix of burly trucker types and leather-clad bikers who jammed the curb outside with Harleys. Tattoos were common, even among the few women who ventured in. Your choice of refreshment was limited to hard liquor or Pabst Blue Ribbon beer and, aside from an old pool table in the back, the only entertainment was a jukebox that played nothing but country music. And not what passes for country these days. There was no Shania Twain, no Garth Brooks or Wynonna. Only Johnny Cash and Waylon Jennings, Merle Haggard and Patsy Cline.

At first sight the Coyote is a bit of a shock, but if you can resist the instinct to flee you soon realize that the bar is a gem, a shrine—one of those extraordinary displays of raw humanity, the witnessing of which is worth the clouds of secondhand smoke you suck down and the risk of physical injury.

I mention injury because fights were not uncommon. But rather than stepping in to stop them, the other men in the bar would just let those involved go at it until some kind of new understanding or equilibrium was established. In fact, most wouldn't even acknowledge the disturbance, turning around only if they were mistakenly jostled by one of the combatants, or if the sound of a breaking bottle or smashing chair interrupted their conversation.

"It's a good thing," a bear of a man grunted at me once, having noticed my horrified expression as I watched two bikers throw each other over tabletops. "Clears the air."

It was as if a roadhouse saloon on some country highway deep in Mississippi or Alabama had been uprooted, flown north by helicopter, and dropped down, of all places, on the Lower East Side of Manhattan. And Ted and I loved it.

"I've got an interview tomorrow with *Business Week*," he explained after we'd claimed a booth and started our first can of Pabst. Ted preferred pitchers, but I was hoping that cans would help me pace myself and honor, however lamely, my pledge to avoid alcohol. I would have ordered soda, but was certain the Coyote had none. And the request might have gotten me killed.

"Really? To do what?"

"I'd be running their Tokyo bureau."

"That's terrific."

"It would be," he said. "Responsibility for a major bureau at this stage in my career is unusual. I'm lucky they're even talking to me. Of course, I had to come ten thousand miles for the damn interview."

"They're paying for it, aren't they?"

Ted nodded, lowering his beer to the table. "They even flew Carrie over with me."

"She's in town, too?"

Ted shook his head. "She went to see her parents on Long Island."

"So how's life in Japan?"

"It's good. A little slow going at first, but this interview could change that."

"Carrie liking it?"

"Loves it. She's working at a museum and doing research for a guy who's apparently one of the leading authorities in her field. He ran across her dissertation last year on the Internet and got in touch with her. Plus, being in Japan is kind of a homecoming for her."

"Oh, that's right, she went to . . . what was it? High school there?"

Ted grinned. "You've got a good memory."

Ted and Carrie had been married for three years. They'd met at Columbia where we had all lived on the eleventh floor of a dormitory called Johnson Hall. There were maybe ten of us on the floor, all in different programs, who, over the course of that first year, became friends.

They kept it to themselves as long as they could, fearing, I guess, that a romance budding within the group would somehow upset the delicate balance of a circle of friends that included men and women. Keeping it undercover was easy at first; the two of them are different enough that no one would have immediately suspected an attraction.

Ted was the third of four sons from a working-class town outside Detroit. He was at the School of Journalism and looked the part: tall and lean, thick bushy hair, wire-rim glasses, fond of sweaters, a rolled-up magazine perpetually stuck in the back pocket of his faded jeans. He was an avid sports fan—the kind who knows names and statistics—and hoped to become a feature writer at a major newspaper. Carrie was the only child of intellectuals and had grown up mostly in Japan, where her father had been a professor of Western literature. That first year in Johnson Hall, she was nearing the end of her course work toward a Ph.D. in art history, specializing in paintings from one of Japan's ancient dynasties. She was the studious sort, quiet and reserved and slightly uppity—she found sports cretinous or at best a bore—but was petite and pretty, with shoulder-length brown hair and deep brown eyes.

We all eventually figured it out, of course. Ted and Carrie probably knew that we knew, but still chose not to let on. What gave them away finally was the fire alarm.

The alarm in the dorm went off all the time, sometimes two or three times a week, and usually in the middle of the night. We never determined whether the cause was the building's aging wiring or an undergraduate prankster. Whatever the reason, no matter what time of night, everyone had to pull themselves out of bed and file cloudy-headed and cursing down the eleven flights of stairs to gather in the cold courtyard in front of the building. A neighbor down the hall once protested the repeated inconvenience by staying in bed and had his door broken down by the firemen.

One night in early December the alarm sounded at three in the morning. Slowly the hall filled with sleepy, angry graduate students.

"If I ever catch the asshole doing this, I'll fuckin' kill him," my next-door neighbor grumbled, standing in his slippers and parka and fumbling with his keys.

I looked down the hall toward Ted's room. "Where's O'Connell?"

Just then, at the other end of the hall, Carrie's door opened and out they walked.

Downstairs, huddling in our sweatshirts and bathrobes while the firemen determined, once again, that the alarm was false, no one said a word. Then, sensing that it was time, or maybe realizing how obvious it all was, Ted slipped his arm around Carrie's waist and, leaning forward, gently kissed the nape of her neck. It was a simple gesture, but those of us monitoring the situation realized its significance. It was an event, a public declaration. Shocked, Carrie recoiled from Ted's kiss, but it was too late. The other eight or ten of us burst into applause, thoroughly embarrassing Carrie and delighting Ted to the point of laughter. With the rest of us looking on, he grabbed Carrie and kissed her hard on the lips, to which we responded by cheering even louder. It was all very happy and I remember being glad for Ted.

"So what about you?" he asked. "You've become a real New Yorker."

I nodded, frowned. "Still at the bank. Same old thing."

"Doing any writing?"

"Some, but it's hard with the distractions of the job."

"Quit."

"Right," I said.

Ted fingered his can for a moment. "So, uh . . . who's this Sarah?"

I was stunned. I'd only known Sarah for three weeks and had not communicated with Ted in months. "How do you know about Sarah?"

"Japan's not that far away, Jack."

I studied him. "And Alex has a big mouth." I'd introduced Ted and Alex years before.

Ted grinned. "So who is she?"

"We're not seeing each other," I said, reaching for my beer.

Ted slumped back in the booth, as if shoved by my answer. "I thought you just met her."

"Three weeks ago."

"Who is she?"

"You remember Janie Marino? Was at the B-school with me?"

"Yeah, sure."

"Her boyfriend Matt is Sarah's brother."

"That's how you met her?"

I shook my head. "I went to the wedding of a college friend last month out in Jersey. Met her at the reception. She and the bride went to high school together."

Ted laughed. "Small world."

I nodded.

"So what's her story?"

"Lawyer here in town," I sighed. I was tiring of his inter-rogation. And didn't like the drift of the conversation.

"Cute?"

"Very attractive."

"She sounds great."

"She's fine."

"And?"

I looked at him flatly. "Let's talk about something else."

Ted gave a frustrated chuckle. I looked at him across the table. He sat looking back at me, his eyebrows raised inquis-itively.

"I'm not looking for a relationship right now," I said.

"What does that mean?"

"It means exactly that. I don't want a woman in my life. Don't need it, don't want it."

"So you broke it off."

"There was nothing to break off."

"But you went out with her, right?"

"Yeah, once."

"You didn't like her?"

"She was fine," I said.

"She was fine."

"Yes."

"But you're not going to call her back."

"Can we move on?"

"I'm just wondering what happened. She was fine, she's attractive and smart . . . but you're not going to call her back. Doesn't add up."

"Like I said, I don't want to be in a relationship at the moment."

"And you're sure she does."

I paused a moment. "I think she's looking for something I can't give her right now."

"She likes you," he said.

"Yes, I think she likes me." I frowned. "Or she did, anyway."

"*Well!*" Ted said suddenly, smacking his palms on the table. "Why didn't you say so? That explains everything!" His tone had turned sarcastic. "No wonder you broke it off. I mean, after all, a woman *liking* you or, God forbid, actually having real feelings for you, well—that's the kiss of death for Jack Lafferty!"

I was peeved, but said nothing. I hadn't seen Ted in two years and hoped that, having made the remark and taken his shot at me, he'd just let it go.

But he persisted. "That's it, isn't it?"

I sipped my beer.

"I'm right, aren't I?"

I looked over at him. The familiar I-know-you-too-well grin was plastered on his face. I'd always hated that grin. "That's ridiculous," I said, trying to swallow the burn in my chest.

"No, Jack," he laughed. "*You're* ridiculous."

I looked over at him again. He was giving me the same stupid smile. Then he laughed again and shook his head, as if I was totally predictable. Or absolutely hopeless.

He was right, of course, and it was his dead-on ability to expose me that made him a good friend and, at times, made me hate him. The truth was that, for whatever reasons, before I'd met Kim, it had been happening the same way for years, woman after woman, always the same.

Not that I'd been serious with every woman I'd run across. There were the usual brief affairs, silly adolescent flings, both of us knowing that it was a short-lived, mostly physical thing that in the end was always easy to walk away from. But with the others, those I'd call relationships, it had always been the same. There was Brenda, freshman year of college, my first real romance; then Laura, junior into senior year; Marlena, the reporter that year in Washington after graduation; Leslie in graduate school; Cynthia, the advertising executive. All very different women with nothing much in common—except that they were all attractive, good women who eventually reached the point of simply wanting to be with me. That's when I lost interest.

That any of them had come to feel something real for me was always a little surprising. Though I tried to be attentive and affectionate, and presumably was fun to be with, I was nevertheless aloof—willing to let them in only so far, and never allowing them to see or experience all of me. It wasn't a game I played or some sick control thing. I'd just never been taken with anyone enough to want to give it all away. It just hadn't happened. I'd never gone to pieces over a woman and, maybe for that reason, had always been suspicious of men who did.

It wasn't that I didn't want it to happen. I did. I wanted to be swept away. Wanted to be hopeless and stupid for someone. Wanted to be able to walk into a restaurant or bar filled with beautiful women yet have my eyes and attention locked firmly on her, hanging on her every word and thought, and looking forward to the end of the evening when I'd take her home and wrap myself breathless and happy around her, body and soul. I believed that could happen and even hoped that it would. It just never had. I'd never met a woman who could do that to me. Who could hold my attention and continue to fascinate and intrigue me. Whose intensity of spirit, intellect, and charm backed me away from a table. Who without even trying could somehow break through and shake me, leaving me unable to think about anything but her. Leaving me thinking, knowing, that I couldn't live without her.

The closest I'd come to that kind of aching desperation was sex. That point making love when suddenly your bodies and minds collapse together and it's no longer just a physical indulgence, but an act of escape and renewal. When for no real reason the tears come and despite the reaching and grasping and holding and thrusting you just can't get close enough.

But what I'd never understood, and what I'd spent years mourning and trying to bend my brain around, is how that kind of rapture can happen and then, later, with the very same person, go cold. Monogamy and passion seemed to be nullifying forces, one enveloping and obliterating the other, leaving the good but passion-hungry person with a horrifying choice.

For a long while I thought the thing to do was to seek out and indulge in as much passion as possible, as if I could somehow accumulate a store of experiences and memories that would sustain me through the rest of my life as a married monogamous man. But my experiences never seemed to overtake or outpace my hunger for the heady rush of the fresh and new, and I soon realized that the hoarding of a surplus that could be drawn down as needed over a lifetime was impossible.

I was back at the same apparent fork in the road: monogamy or passion. Stability or freedom. Somehow I just couldn't square one with the other and, needing to, I hadn't been able to commit to any one woman—or even to seriously consider doing so.

Until Kim. And what had that gotten me?

The bar was crowded now, the decibel level higher, but I could still make out the Man in Black:

You'd say the same old thing
you've been saying all along.
Lay there in your bed
and keep your mouth shut 'til I'm gone.
Don't give me that old familiar cryin', cussin' moan . . .
Understand your man.

I'd lost patience with Ted's appraising stare. "What?"

"What do you think you're looking for?"

I'd had it. "Look," I said, smacking my beer can on the table more loudly than I'd intended, "it's good to see you. It really is. But this conversation has grown tedious, okay? Let's move on."

"It's just that you intrigue me."

"What's so intriguing?" I asked peevishly. "Am I really such an oddity?"

"Well, I can't figure you. I mean, I can't imagine what it is you're looking for." He pulled his elbows onto the table. "I've known you a long time. Long enough to have met most of the women you've dated, and all of them have been terrific catches. Beautiful, smart, ambitious. And this Sarah sounds the same. Most guys would be thrilled to end up with any one of them."

"Guess I'm not most guys," I said.

"Clearly not. And that's okay. But it leaves me wondering

what you're looking for." He turned and looked out over the bar, his face pinching into an odd expression, as if carefully putting together his next thought. After a moment, he looked back at me, his eyes narrowed. "Are you sure you're meant to be with a woman?"

I stared at him. "You're *not* asking me if I'm gay."

"Well," he said, waving his hands in the air, "it's not beyond the realm of possibility."

"Yes it is," I said emphatically.

"All right," he said, holding up his palms in apology. "Just thought we should cover that base."

"We don't need to be covering *any* bases," I said, my patience reaching its limits. "You're not my shrink and I don't need therapy. I don't have to be married or in a relationship to be considered healthy." I sat back in the booth, slammed a gulp of beer, then lurched forward again. "You know what I think this is about?" I said, jabbing a finger at him. "You're jealous."

"I'm jealous."

"Absolutely. All my married friends want me to be married. 'When are you getting married, Jack?' 'How come you're not married yet, Jack?' And I know exactly why. Misery loves company."

Ted laughed.

"Admit it," I said. "You can't stand it that I can still do whatever I want, or ask out whoever I want."

"Look," he said, shaking his head, "I'll admit that I look back on my single days fondly and that I'm amused by the stories you and Alex tell. But I'm not jealous of you. I'm a happily married man. I'm also your friend and I worry about you."

"I'm touched."

"Don't be pissed off, Jack. We're just talking. I didn't say you have to be married to be healthy. It's just that you seem so against the idea."

"I'm not against it," I protested. "I was *engaged!*"

"That's true," he said, nodding. "Definitely true. But for years all these great women just passed through your life and you never seemed particularly taken with any of them. And now it's the same with this Sarah. From what Alex tells me, she's really something special."

"I just haven't met the right one yet," I said flatly.

Ted studied me across the table.

A burst of loud laughter came suddenly from across the room and I used it as an excuse to look away. A group of men were gathered around the pool table in the back of the room. One of them, a tall, rough-looking man in jeans and a worn leather jacket, was receiving applause and backslaps from the others. The man, still holding his pool cue, raised a can of Pabst in the smoky air to acknowledge their congratulations.

"Must have made a great shot," Ted said.

I stole a quick glance at him. He sat with his hands on the table in front of him, fumbling with his fingernails. Then suddenly: "Have you ever been in love?"

"For Christ's sake!"

"Well, have you?"

"This is stupid."

"It's just a question," he said, protesting my exasperation. "I'm not asking if you've ever stolen anything or tried heroin. I'm just curious if you've ever been in love."

I threw up my hands. "I don't know."

"How can you not know?"

I shook my head.

"How can you not know?" he said again.

"Yes!" I nearly shouted. "Okay? Yes, I loved Kim. I mean, *obviously*. I'd be married now if she hadn't —" I looked away for a moment. "I loved Kim."

"And now you're afraid to love someone else."

"Is this the fucking *Oprah* show?"

"It scares you."

I frowned. "It doesn't *scare* me. And I hate how everyone always talks about it in those terms. You're *afraid* of intimacy. You're a commitment-*phobe*. That's such bullshit. I've never been *afraid* of commitment. It just always, you know . . . worried me."

"What're you worried about?"

"That I'll go ahead and do it, get married and start a life with someone, and then one day, maybe a month later or ten years later, I'll find her. I'm working with her, or we'll meet at a party, or she'll stand next to me on the bus. I'll look into her face and she'll smile and I'll know. But I won't be able to do anything about it. It'll be too late. I'll already be married. I mean, look what happened with Kim. I thought I knew her and— Well, obviously I didn't."

"Lightning bolts only happen in movies," Ted said. "Not in real life."

"I think they do happen, and that's what worries me."

"Has it ever happened to you before?"

"Not yet."

"Then why do you think it ever will?"

I shrugged. "You have to believe in something."

"I'd pick something else to believe in," he said.

"I like believing in lightning bolts."

"You're not getting any younger, Jack."

"I'm male," I said. "Thirty-five is young."

"How long does it seem since you were twenty?"

I reached for my beer.

"Pretty soon you realize that you better invest in something. Take a chance or you'll end up alone."

I was appalled. "So *that's* why people get married? To escape being alone? That's a pretty pathetic reason to commit to someone for the rest of your life."

"Well, that's more or less what it comes down to in the end. I mean, of course you have to like being with the person. You can't pick just anybody. But don't think you'll stay crazy in love forever. Don't think that every time Carrie and I have sex it's as hot and desperate as the first few times I snuck into her room in Johnson Hall. It fades."

"That's really terrific news, Ted."

"Well, it's true. Life's not all passion and romance. Ultimately you get married because you want some company along the way."

"I'd rather be alone," I said. "It's not so bad."

"You look like you're really enjoying your freedom tonight," he said.

"Temporary setback."

"A temporary setback of loneliness between the lofty peaks of unsuccessful relationships and meaningless conquests. Those are pretty pathetic reasons for putting off a girl whose only crime is that she might want to be with you."

I looked hard at him. "You're a goddamn philosopher now?"

"No, I've just evolved to the point where I'm happy with one woman."

"Well, congratulations. And don't give me that *I've evolved* crap, like I'm some kind of emotional Neanderthal."

"Sorry. Look at it this way—what's the worst thing that can happen? A few years down the road you hate each other, or your Hollywood lightning bolt strikes, and you find someone you like better. So you get divorced. People do it all the time."

I pulled my elbow onto the table, pointed a finger at him. "You know, the irony here is that I take marriage a lot more seriously than you do."

He laughed.

"It's true. I don't want to get into it only to then get out if things don't work or I find someone else. I want it to be for real when I do it. You know, the love of my life and all that. I don't want to do it until I'm sure."

"But you won't be."

"Won't be what?"

"Sure. That's the fallacy in your thinking. You're never really sure."

"That's bullshit. I know a lot of people, my parents included, who say they absolutely knew."

"They're lying."

I tossed my head.

"They're lying," he said again.

"What do you *mean* they're lying?"

"I mean, they like to think they were sure because it's fun to think that way. And because it makes getting through life honoring their commitment easier. But the truth is you're never really sure."

"You're not sure you love Carrie?"

"That's not what I said. I know I love Carrie. I'm just saying that no one has a crystal ball and you don't know how it will go. It's a risk. It's the rest of your life."

"Exactly. And the rest of your life is a long damn time and I'd prefer to spend it happy. So I want to be sure."

"But you won't be, Jack. It's a risk. A leap. That's the nature of the thing. That's what it's about."

"Well, then that's my problem," I said. "I don't like risks."

"No one does. But that's how you know you're ready."

"What do you mean?"

"If there were no risk to it, there'd be no way to gauge how you really feel. Right? It would be a purely rational act and too easy to make a mistake. Risk is essential to the exercise. To focus your feelings. Clarify your thinking. You know you're ready and that you've found the right girl when, in spite of the risk, you still want to do it. When the idea of risking the rest of your life with this one girl is actually kind of cool." He smiled. "Risk isn't your problem, Jack. It's your friend. You're a banker," he said. "You should understand that."

I looked at him hard, then shook my head. "Sounds like insanity to me."

He laughed. "We need more beer."

He got up and walked over to the bar. I watched him go, and as he reached the counter I noticed one of the bartenders for the first time—a young woman in her mid-twenties, at the other end of the bar. She was medium height but lean, with long legs, small, rounded breasts, and athletic but thoroughly feminine shoulders. Her face was softly angular, and her dirty blond hair was cropped just below her ears, giving her a sassy, tomboyish look that fit with her jeans and the sleeveless denim shirt she wore tied in a knot at her waist.

She was beautiful, and as I watched a smile light up her face I felt the familiar darkness rising within me. I wanted this girl. I wanted to know that body. To feel that pretty skin pressed against me. To smell and to taste her. And it suddenly occurred to me that what I needed wasn't a new relationship, or even a new view of relationships. I needed to get laid. Alex was right. I needed some good, old-fashioned, hot and sweaty, wreck-the-bed sex. I needed some carnal therapy. I needed sexual healing.

As I watched the girl behind the bar, I imagined her in my bed. Her brown body against my white sheets, lying on her tummy, arms up by her head. I would start at her neck, at the hairline, slipping lightly down and then up each side and nipping at her ears, drawing little giggles between the quiet gasps. I would linger at her shoulders, moving slowly and softly across one side and over to the other, then down between the delicate shoulder blades. My mouth would follow my fingertips down her spine to the small of her back, across her hips, and down over the final heartbreaking curve of her to the backs of her thighs. Then, rolling her over, I would take in the full sight of her: long legs open and bent at the knees, tummy soft and brown, full round breasts lifting and dropping, lips wet and parted, eyes shining intense and desperate.

And then we would go. First slowly and sweetly and tenderly, then deeply and wantonly and maddeningly. We'd go together and go alone, she in me and me in her and we together in ourselves and in each other, all powerful and all helpless, reaching and clinging and hoping and holding tightly, ever tightly, as if to life itself. As if somewhere in the chaos and delirious passion lay hidden the meaning of all our worldly suffering and the promise of all our dreams. How did Kerouac describe it? *The sweetest, the most pure and delicious joy two people can experience together on this earth.* Something like that. Anyway, he was right. He knew.

"Jack?"

"Hmmm?"

"Still here?"

"Sorry," I said, still watching the girl behind the bar.

Ted turned his head and followed the path of my gaze. "Forget it," he said, turning back to me.

"She's pretty."

"She's gorgeous, but it's a no-chancer."

"I bet she's southern," I said. "Texas, maybe Georgia."

Ted turned and looked at the girl again. "Why?"

"Something about her," I said, watching her smile again. "The way she looks, the way she moves. Something casual about her. Plus she works here, in a place that serves Pabst and plays country music."

"She's probably from Scarsdale," Ted said.

I shook my head, still looking at the girl. "Don't think so. There's something different about her. I think I'll ask her."

"Don't be stupid."

I flexed my eyebrows at him.

"Do you know how many come-ons a girl like that must get each night in this bar? You'll be just another swinging dick looking for a place to park."

"At least that's the honest truth," I said. "I'm tired of playing games."

"She'll crucify you, Jack. Forget it."

"I'll be right back," I said, standing up.

Ted sank back in the booth, covering his face with his hand.

The girl was at the tap filling a pitcher. "What can I get you?" she asked as I reached the bar.

"Two Pabst," I said.

The girl nodded and, turning from the tap still pouring into the pitcher, pulled two cans of beer from an ice-filled bathtub tucked under the back counter. "Four dollars," she said, dropping the beers on the bar. She was even more beautiful up close. I slid six dollars onto the bar.

"I bet you're from down south," I said with a smile.

The girl's eyes slid sideways. "What?"

"I was just wondering if you're from down south. You seem like you would be."

"What makes you think that?"

I shrugged, grinning again. "Just a hunch."

"I'm from L.A.," she said flatly, her attention turning to a second pitcher.

"L.A.? Well, that's *southern* California," I said. "Guess I can let that count. So what's your name, Miss Southern California?"

"Go fuck yourself." With that, she hoisted the two pitchers, one handle in each pretty fist, and walked down the length of the bar.

"What'd she say?" Ted asked as I dropped the cans of Pabst onto the table and fell into my side of the booth.

"She's not southern."

"No?"

"L.A."

"Really?"

"She told me to go fuck myself."

Ted threw his head back and laughed.

I was quiet.

"I warned you," he said, still laughing.

I was on my feet again.

"Where're you going?"

"Be right back."

"Jack . . . Jack, are you *insane*?"

The girl was at the tap again, filling yet another pitcher. Seeing me approach, she lowered her eyes and shook her head. You do what you have to do, say what you have to say. This girl was far too savvy, too cynical, for a line about being southern to work. I had to change tactics. I would use the honesty approach. It had nothing to do with honesty or reality, of course. It was about making the score. Getting a name or a phone number. I would simply tell her that I thought she was beautiful and that I just wanted to meet her. Insanely straightforward, and that was the point. In my experience the honesty approach had been remarkably effective, if delivered properly. Revealing yourself, or at least appearing to, is disarming and unsettling. You show your hand and she feels obliged to do the same. Or at least to acknowledge your gesture. Only a truly cruel woman could crush you after the honesty approach. Reaching the bar, I put my palms on the counter.

"You're back," she said without looking at me.

I nodded.

"What part of 'go fuck yourself' do you not understand?"

"Look," I began, letting my voice go flat with resignation, "I didn't mean to embarrass you or make you feel uncomfortable." I shrugged casually, penitently. "I just wanted to meet you, okay? I saw you over here, you're very attractive, and I thought I'd like to know you. That's all. Sorry if I made you uncomfortable."

Then I gave her the smile. The one you do more with the eyes than the lips. The smile that conveys a sincere apology— or a subtle but unmistakable appeal for intimacy. I delivered it as powerfully as I could, as I had a hundred other times to a hundred other women, then turned and began walking back to the table.

"Hey, hold on!" I heard from behind me. Her tone was harsh, even angry. I turned to find her facing me, hands on her hips. Raising her right hand, she beckoned me with a few quick curls of her index finger. I took a few steps toward her, struggling to maintain a vacant, uninterested expression.

"Just curious," she said. "Does that crap work with most women?"

I shrugged. "Nearly always."

"You're kidding."

I shook my head.

She dried her hands on the towel tucked into the waist of her jeans, looking me over. "What's your name?"

"Jack," I said, reaching out over the bar.

But she didn't move; she just stood there, drying her hands, studying me.

"Oh, come on," I said. "This isn't easy, you know."

She continued to stare. Then, slowly, as if against her better judgment, she reached for my hand. "Alison," she said, and we both felt the jolt of first touch.

"Nice to meet you, Alison."

"Sorry I was nasty to you," she said. "A girl has to be careful." She reclaimed her hand, then stepped back over to the tap and tugged the handle, shooting a stream of golden beer into the waiting pitcher.

"Have dinner with me sometime and I'll think about for-giving you."

She gave a derisive chuckle. "I really don't care if you for-give me."

"Can I call you?"

She shot a you-must-be-joking look, then hoisted the froth-ing pitcher and walked down to the far end of the bar.

I waited, watching as she filled the orders of several bearded, leathered hulks.

Finally turning away from the cash register, she looked my way. "Still here?"

"Have dinner with me sometime."

"You can't be serious."

"Of course I'm serious. Is it so wrong that I'd like to buy you dinner? Don't I look trustworthy?" I looked over my shoulder, then back to her. "Or would you rather I weighed a hundred more pounds, dressed in leather, had tattoos up and down my arms, and hadn't bathed in a week?"

She laughed. "Better be careful, yuppie boy," she said, nod-ding to the room behind me.

"Come on, Alison. You work at the Coyote. How bad could I be?"

"I like the Coyote."

"I love the Coyote," I said. "I've been coming here for years."

"I've never seen you in here before."

"I came a lot when I was in grad school," I said. "That was ten years ago."

She looked me over for another moment, then gave a weary sort of smirk. Pulling a pen from a pocket, she scribbled a number on a napkin, then tossed the napkin into a puddle on the bar. "Don't keep me waiting," she said.

I stuffed the damp napkin into my pocket, then reached over the bar. "I won't."

Leaving my outstretched hand hovering in the air, Alison from L.A. turned and walked away.

Back at the table, Ted sat wearing an expression of genuine amazement. "A remarkable recovery, Jack," he said as I sat down. "I have to say, that was truly brilliant. One for the books."

"Elementary, my dear Watson."

"You got her number?"

I nodded.

"You gonna call her?"

"Maybe."

We finished our beers and decided to leave. The smoke was killing us. Outside, as Ted slipped on his jacket, I turned and looked up at the neon lettering over the door. "What the hell does that mean, anyway?"

"What?"

"'Coyote ugly.'"

"You've heard that before."

"I've heard of it. I know this bar and know about the movie. It's the term, the expression I don't get. You're as ugly as a coyote?"

"No, that's not it," he said. We started up the sidewalk together. "When a coyote gets caught in one of those steel traps that hunters set up in the woods," he went on, "they'll chew off their foot to get away. Other animals will just lie there and die, but coyotes will maim themselves to stay free."

"Okay . . ."

"So 'coyote ugly' refers to the appearance of the girl you wake up with the morning after a night of serious drinking. Your arm is caught under her head. But she's so damn ugly that you'd rather chew off your arm to get away than risk waking her up."

I laughed. "That's so *harsh*!"

We walked a few more blocks together, then I asked Ted if he wanted to stop at another bar for a last drink. He shook his head.

"But it's still early," I protested. "And we've only had a few beers."

"I can't," he said. "I've got to get back to the hotel. Have to call Carrie before it gets too late."

I frowned at him. "Such a good husband."

"Responsibilities," he said.

"Well, it was good seeing you."

"Likewise," he said, taking my hand firmly. "Come visit Tokyo. You'd like it."

"Let me know how the interview goes."

He nodded. Then, giving my hand a final squeeze, he said: "Don't be a coyote, Jack."

"Very funny."

"I'm serious. It's no way to live."

"Lying there in the trap and dying is better?"

"Marriage isn't a trap," he said. "In fact, studies show that married men live longer, happier, healthier lives than single men."

"Studies done by married scientists, I'll bet."

Ted rolled his eyes.

"Take care," I said.

He gave me a frowning sort of smile, then waved, jumped in the back of a cab, and was gone.

Riding uptown on the 2 train, I thought of the girl. I smiled to myself. It had been a good night. I'd gotten what I wanted. I had the phone number of a beautiful girl in my pocket. In no time, a couple of weeks, maybe less, she would be in my bed. Smooth and brown and lovely against my white sheets. Her body wanting and open and reaching for me with long legs and soft arms and warm mouth. It had been a good night.

As the train howled through the Twenty-third Street station, I thought about Ted back in his hotel room, calling his wife to say good night and that he missed her. I laughed to myself. How fucking cute. Running back to call the little woman. The same woman he'll be calling for the rest of his life. The same voice on the other end of the phone. The same voice, the same woman, the same body—for the rest of his time on the planet!

My back pressed hard against the wall of the car as the train swung right and onto the thirty-block run from Forty-second to Seventy-second Street. Coming out of the turn, the train accelerated, steel wheels screaming against iron tracks, my car rocking and moaning. The local stations flew by in a white blur of fluorescent lighting, ceramic tiles, and vertical support beams. I felt the rush of speed. I felt the rush of freedom. I could take that train anywhere I wanted. Do anything I wanted. There was no one I had to get home to, no one I had to call. I was on my own, free and wild and young—*still young!*—in New York City! And I had the number of a gorgeous girl in my pocket.

I thought about the girl. What was her name? Alison?

That's right, Alison. God, she was beautiful. Alex would approve. Alex would be fucking thrilled. And it had been perfect. Ted was right. One for the books. A couple of weeks. Maybe less.

I felt good about it. About not giving up. About going back and getting the number. I felt exhilarated. I felt free. I felt like a man.

I'll be as gone as a wild goose in winter, and then you'll . . .
Understand your man.
Meditate on that, honey.
Understand your man . . .

Chapter 13

But by the time I woke the next morning—cotton-mouthed and feeling even the few cans of Pabst I'd allowed myself— the enthusiasm, the élan, I'd felt so completely the evening before had dissipated. I was still glad to have gotten Alison's number. Glad I'd hung in there, adapting to circumstances, shifting strategies, and ultimately, triumphantly, achieving the objective. The score felt good. But whatever temporary thrill I'd experienced, whatever boost to my confidence I'd achieved, the dull throb in my head as I lay staring at the ceiling seemed a monotonous refrain of my undiminished quandary: Alison, like Sarah, like Kim, like all the rest of them, was, however magnificent, however delicious, still a woman. And I, of course, was still a man. Those inescapable facts, and the complexities and complications I knew would inevitably set in, had, at last, tragically, robbed me even of my enthusiasm for whatever momentary rapture Alison and

I might share by desperately mingling our physical differences.

In despair, I rolled over and did the only thing that any man—frustrated, defeated, and cynical, with nowhere else to turn—could do. I called my father.

I'd never really talked to my father about women. There never seemed to be much point. My father is a man who married the first woman he ever slept with—and he slept with her *after* he married her. The fact that he's been married longer than I've been on the planet never seemed to matter. I considered my mother a single data point, a lone observation, from which no meaningful conclusions could be drawn. Still, with nothing to lose, and looking for another ear to bend, I called home.

"I just don't understand them," I declared after ten minutes of ranting.

My father laughed. "And you never will, Jack."

"Really?" I said, resisting the prospect of eternal torture. "Why does it have to be that way? I mean, why does the whole goddamn business have to be so difficult?"

"Why can't a woman be more like a man?"

"Well, exactly."

"You remember what that's from?"

"Yes," I sighed. *"My Fair Lady."* My father is a lover of the Broadway musicals of the forties and fifties—America's Golden Age, he insists. My memories of childhood echo with the words and music of Rodgers and Hammerstein, Lerner and Loewe, and George and Ira Gershwin.

"Henry Higgins wasn't the first man to ask that question," my father said, "and you won't be the last."

"I seem to recall another of Professor Higgins's lines," I said. "'Let a woman in your life, and you invite eternal strife.'"

"Oh, come on, Jack. New York has turned you into a cynic."

"New York *women*," I corrected him.

He laughed again. "Look, do you remember Higgins's final thoughts on the matter? 'I've grown accustomed to her face . . .'" He was singing now. "'She almost makes the day begin . . .'"

"Don't sing, Dad."

"All right, I won't torture you. But do you remember the last stanza?"

"I think I've repressed it."

"'I'm very grateful she's a woman and so easy to forget,'" he recited, ignoring my objection. "'Rather like a habit one can always break. *And yet . . .*'" Again he sang: "'I've grown accustomed to the trace . . . of something in the air. Accustomed . . . to her . . . face.'"

"Very inspiring, Dad."

"I'm glad you liked it."

"I can't believe you're giving me advice based on show tunes."

"The point, son, is the word *something*. Something, as in mystery." Life is full of riddles and mysteries, he said. It's important to know the difference.

"Which is?"

"Riddles have answers," he said. "They're meant to be figured out. Mysteries aren't. They don't have answers. Not for us, anyway."

"So, you're saying women fall into the mystery category and I'm just torturing myself trying to figure them out."

"I'm saying you don't want to figure them out."

He said my generation thinks too much. That we're products of the information age. We think every question has an answer, every problem a clear solution, just as long as we pull together enough information and think hard enough about it. But when it comes to relationships there's never enough information. Never utter clarity. And our persistent searching for perfection is pointless and dispiriting.

"That's why you folks are getting married later and later," he said. "You're commitment-phobes because you don't understand commitment. And I'm not talking about the sticking-to-it part. I mean the very nature of it. What it's about."

"Maybe we're just being careful."

"Maybe," he said. "But by being so careful, I think many of you are cheating yourselves."

"How so?"

"If perfect understanding was possible, Jack, what would be the point of commitment?" What makes commitment important, he said, what gives it value and meaning, is that you're signing on to something without complete information. You're trusting in something beyond yourself, beyond your own understanding and control.

Exactly, I said. That's why it's so frightening.

"It is a little scary," he conceded. "But even if perfect understanding were possible, trust me, you wouldn't want it."

Life is about muddling through, he said. About figuring out ways to make the imperfect workable. Mystery gives life color and texture. I shouldn't rob myself of that pleasure, that joy, by beating my head against the wall, he said. Then, returning to the original topic: "Look, men and women are more alike than different. But clearly we differ in profound ways. And thank God for that. Life would be awfully stark if we were all the same."

"It would be a lot simpler," I said.

"Simpler isn't always better, son."

"So, exactly what fatherly wisdom are you imparting?"

"Just let go," he said. Give in. Surrender. Appreciate the mystery for what it is. "Variety is the spice of life," he said, a smile in his voice. "*Vive la différence!*"

Some part of what my father was saying seemed right; I felt it resonate in my heart and mind. But the sensation felt too much like the sudden delight, the giddy relief, of finding out that the exam you're unprepared for has been put off. His advice, however appealing, seemed too easy, too dismissive. It smacked of cop-out—the limited knowledge of a man with limited experience.

And his simple take on the complex topic was pretty much the kind of thing I expected to hear from him. One must, after all, justify one's own choices and decisions, one's own station in life.

Disappointed, I thanked him for his thoughts and said good-bye.

Chapter 14

I was at home working on a new story when my phone rang.

It was Alex. He asked if I could meet for a drink. He sounded odd. Troubled. I asked if everything was all right. Yes, he was fine, he said, but when could we meet? I figured something had happened with Karen.

It was a spectacular evening as I left my apartment, unusually cool with a delightful breeze that smelled fresh and wonderful. It had been a hot, miserable summer and the sidewalk was crowded with people out strolling, looking in shopwindows, enjoying the unseasonable, almost spring-like weather.

As I approached the restaurant I could see Alex standing out front, waiting for me, arms folded across his chest. I smiled and waved. He gave a stiff wave back. We decided to sit outside, chose a table by the railing, closest to the crowd passing by on the sidewalk. A waitress appeared and took our order with a bright, easy smile. I watched her as she walked away.

Alex and I shared small talk for several minutes, both of us understanding that we would wait for our drinks before broaching whatever subject we'd met to discuss. We commented on the weather, reported that work was going well, although very busy.

Our waitress reappeared and set a pint before Alex, a ginger ale before me. I watched again as she walked away, the swell and curve of her hips bouncing nicely beneath her snug skirt. I took a long first swallow, felt it run smooth and cool through my chest. "So," I said finally, "what's on your mind?"

Alex looked at me, then at the tabletop; his lips pressed together, his jaw stiffened; he straightened in his chair. It was clear that whatever news he'd brought was not easy for him to report. I braced myself. He breathed deeply and then: "I'm losing my hair," he declared.

I wasn't sure I'd heard correctly. "What?"

"I'm losing my hair," he said again.

"You think you're losing your *hair*?"

"I don't *think* I'm losing it. I know I am."

I was puzzled. "Is this what you wanted to talk about?"

"Yes."

"Your hair."

"Yes."

I gave a disbelieving chuckle, shook my head.

"What?" he asked indignantly.

"Well"—I snorted again; I couldn't help it—"it's just that when you called you sounded upset. I thought you had something important you wanted to —"

"It *is* important," he interrupted, his face tight, his eyes hard, "and I am *very* upset about it."

I studied him for a moment. I could see that, indeed, he was quite serious—and annoyed that I seemed not to appreciate the gravity of what he was sharing with me. I decided I should play along. "Why do you think you're losing your hair?"

His jaw stiffened again. "I'm telling you it's happening."

I tried again. "Okay, how do you know?"

"It's thinner than it used to be," he said.

"Everyone's hair thins," I said. "It's natural."

"Well, mine is thinning faster than normal."

"Your hair looks exactly the same."

He shook his head. "It's definitely thinner. Even than it was six months ago."

"I think you're imagining it."

"No, I'm not," he insisted. "The signs are there."

"What signs?"

"There's hair in the drain after I shower."

"So?"

"That means it's falling out."

"Not necessarily."

"Is there hair in your drain?"

"I don't know."

"What do you mean you don't know?"

"I mean I have no idea."

"You never glance at the drain when you reach down to turn off the faucet?"

"Not really."

He frowned. "You would if you were losing your hair," he said sullenly.

I took another sip of my soda to conceal a developing smile. "Look," I said, setting the glass on the table again, "I'm sure that when I shower some hair is washed away. That's perfectly normal. Just like when you comb your hair there's some left in the comb. That always happens. I remember my mother would leave enough in the bristles of her brush to cover someone else's head. Everyone is constantly losing some hair, but new hair is always growing in to replace it."

"Right, *normally*," he countered. "But what if it begins falling out faster than it's coming in? That's what is happening. It's a question of degree."

I was losing patience. "So your hair may be thinning a little—"

"So you agree."

"No, I don't agree."

"You just said it's thinning."

"No, I'm just granting your point that—"

"So you agree."

"Alex—"

"You just *said* you're granting the point!" he fairly shouted. "You're conceding the fact! You agree! Just ad*mit* it, for chrissake!"

I was getting angry in a hurry. Feeling it in my throat, I tucked my chin toward my chest, pausing momentarily. "Alex, my concession was meant merely as an acceptance of a hypothetical premise. I'm reluctantly agreeing to argue on your own ridiculous terms." He glared at me suspiciously. "Even if your hair is thinning," I continued slowly, warily, "which in my opinion it's *not*, but even if *you* think it is, thinning hair is something that happens to everyone to some degree. We can't drink like we used to either."

"It's not the same."

"It's exactly the same. When we were in college we could go to a party, get as drunk as we wanted and be up, fresh and in class at eight o'clock the next morning, no problem. Now, if I have more than a couple of beers, I feel it the next day. Your hair isn't as thick as it was when you were nineteen and neither is mine."

"You haven't lost any hair," he said contemptuously.

"Sure, it's thinned a little."

He frowned, unconvinced, took another sip of his beer.

"Alex, your hair looks exactly the way it always has. Really it does."

"It does to you because the damage has been gradual," he said emphatically, returning his glass to the table with a bang. "But I can tell there's not as much."

"Okay, how?" I asked, reduced, finally, to considering the evidence.

Shoving his chair back, he leaned over the table toward me, bowed his head, and with his fingers began separating the hair in the middle of his scalp. "You see that," he said, "you can see my head."

I laughed. "Well, of course I can see your head when you do *that*! You could see anyone's scalp if they pulled their hair apart like that."

"No," he said, sitting back, carefully smoothing his hair with his hand. "It's thinner than it used to be. I mean, when I look around at most men my age, their hair is much fuller." He shook his head sullenly. "I'm losing it."

I'd had enough. "Alex, you're being ridiculous. Paranoid and ridiculous."

At this, he lurched forward in his chair. "When you do

this," he said angrily, quickly pushing his hand, fingers spread apart, through his hair and then, leaning across the table, holding his hand up in front of my face, "does *that* happen?" A few hairs were caught between his fingers.

I pushed his hand away. "Alex, I'm not going to sit here and argue with you about your goddamn hair," I said, thoroughly peeved now. "If you want it to be falling out, then fine, it's falling out."

He sank back in his chair. Shaking my head, I looked away from him and into the street. The sidewalk was very crowded now—people walking their dogs; couples pushing baby strollers; groups of friends sharing stories and laughing. I took another sip of my soda, then glanced across the table at my friend. He sat staring at his glass, spinning it slowly with his fingers.

"Look," I said more gently, "maybe it's thinning, maybe it's not. But even if it is, is it really so important?"

He didn't respond, but only continued to spin the glass between his fingers.

An attractive girl was walking down the sidewalk toward us. I watched her as she approached and passed. "If you're worried about women," I said, "I think most of them realize it happens to some degree to nearly every man. Plus they're not as appearance oriented as we are. They're more enlightened that way. Hell, some women even *prefer* bald men. More skin, I guess."

"It's not that," he said quietly.

"Then what? Why would it bother you so much?"

"Because there's nothing I can do about it."

"That's right, there's nothing *anyone* can do about it," I said, hoping that by acknowledging his powerlessness he could somehow let the anxiety go. But he only shook his head slowly and seemed to sink deeper.

"Jesus, Alex," I said, genuinely astonished. "I really think you're blowing this out of proportion."

"Am I?" he said, looking up from his glass.

"Yes, I really think so."

He studied me a moment, then turned his gaze out over the crowded sidewalk. We sat quietly for a few minutes, watching the people pass by.

"I'm going to be thirty-five this year," he said finally.

"Yeah, so?"

"Thirty-five," he said again, quietly, as if to himself.

"I'm already thirty-five."

"Doesn't it bother you?" he asked, looking back to me.

I shook my head. "Just another number. No more remarkable than any other."

He frowned. "I remember my parents being thirty."

"Really?" I said, without thinking.

He nodded slowly. "I was seven."

Looking across the table into his sad, empty eyes, I suddenly felt the same awkward spasm, the same hollow nausea I often get when peering over the edge of a tall building. He looked into the street again, pensively watching the people pass by. The silly boyish face, usually bright and full of expression, was now dark and drawn. He sat slumped in the chair, one arm pulled tightly across his chest, the other holding his fist under his chin.

"Another round, guys?" asked our waitress who, having noticed that we had reached the bottom of our glasses, had approached from behind me.

I nodded. She smiled down at me and walked away. This

time I didn't watch. There was something different about Alex. Something strange. Something wrong.

Earlier, I compared his penchant for "dude" with Gatsby's "old sport." The parallel, it had occurred to me, didn't end there. Alex wasn't rich, of course. Or stylish or glamorous. Far from it. But if personality really is an unbroken series of successful gestures, there was definitely something about him. Not so much gorgeous as . . . ridiculous. He didn't just believe in the green light, he lived in its warm and verdant glow. He had Gatsby's extraordinary gift for hope, the heightened sensitivity to the promises of life. His wasn't so much a "romantic readiness" as it was an almost comically insistent levity, an absurd sort of optimism.

Life had always seemed so simple to Alex. It was a game, a kind of fun house: the rickety floors, off-kilter walls, and distorting mirrors confused the senses and boggled the mind, but that's what made it fun. You played the experience for what it was and took what you could get. No one got hurt, not really anyway, and it was all a great time. And there wasn't any point in getting too upset about anything. Life had its disappointments, sure, but why waste time dwelling on things you couldn't change when there was a world of new kicks to be had? As he'd said a few nights before in the bar: every day you're another step closer to the grave.

Despite its undeniable elements of truth, this point of view had always struck me as awfully silly. Even sad. I liked Alex, but in that remote, rather reluctant way one likes the class clown—he was amusing, but I can't say that I admired him. He wasn't a thinker, a wonderer, or even particularly curious. He didn't read, listened to bad music, and the closest he came to a cultural experience was eating with chopsticks. He had his own winsome, oddly poetic take on the world—his bizarre one-liners—but it too often seemed lazy and vacuous in its stark simplicity, reducing the mysteries and troubles of life to a kind of manageable shorthand, the logic and insights of which, if indeed there were any, being frequently lost on me. Never once had I known him to hurt over a woman. He was, it seemed to me, a kind of human pinball, ricocheting happily but aimlessly off the bells and bumpers of life.

But what I hadn't understood until that evening—and what came to me, therefore, as something of a shock—was just how much I'd somehow come to rely on that very inanity. Alex and I were different. I was serious, at times too serious. My father was right: I led with my head. And like all such people I suffered needlessly and was often a dreadful bore. Alex, for all his adolescent silliness and unassailable frivolity, provided not only comic relief but also a kind of sanctuary. Hanging out with him was like coming home to one's child after a horrendous day at the office: the burden of one's worries and frustrations dissolved in a warm wash of simple, uncomplicated joy.

And so, sitting stunned across the table from him, I didn't know what to say. There was more to his sudden, inexplicable melancholy than his allegedly thinning hair. There had to be. But as for what the true problem was, I hadn't the first clue. The mere fact that something had finally gotten to him, burrowed into him—and to the extent it apparently had— had me troubled to the point of quiet panic. In fact, I'll admit, it scared the hell out of me.

The waitress returned with our drinks. I thanked her with a nod and a half smile.

Alex was still watching the people on the sidewalk. Then suddenly: "Are you doing what you want to be doing?"

"How do you mean?"

"With your life," he said, his gaze sliding back to me. "Are you doing what you want to be doing?"

"I guess so," I said, shrugging.

"So if you died tomorrow, you'd be satisfied?"

I was horrified. "Alex, what in the world . . . ?"

"I know the question is morbid," he said, holding up an open palm in apology, "but would you die satisfied?"

"No, of course I wouldn't be happy about it," I said, reaching for my glass.

"I didn't say *happy*, I said *satisfied*. Would you be satisfied that you had done the things that you wanted to do in the time you had?"

"Well, no, obviously not," I responded, shifting in my chair. "I haven't accomplished or experienced everything I want to. Haven't had time. I've only been around for thirty-five years."

"I meant something different," he said. "I mean, are you satisfied with what you're doing *now*? At this stage of your life."

"Alex, I'm really not following what you're—"

"Do you ever feel," he interrupted, straightening in his chair again, "that time is beginning to move on you? That you haven't done a lot of the things you'd wanted to do by now, or that you haven't . . ."—waving his hand over the table, groping, it seemed, for the right words—". . . that you haven't found the answers to some of the important questions you thought you'd have figured out by now, and yet your life is getting busier and more complicated every day and distracting more and more of your time and energy away from the things that in the long run, in the end, you'll care about most of all?"

I stared at him, wide-eyed. "Jesus, Alex."

"I'm serious."

"Yeah, no shit."

"I mean, haven't you ever wanted to . . . I don't know, buy a motorcycle, take three months off and drive across the country? You know, some wild, stupid, Jack Kerouac–type thing? Or learn to sail? Or play guitar in some bar band in the Village, or . . . or walk right up to some girl you see on the street, a total stranger, and introduce yourself and tell her you think she's gorgeous and that you'd love to buy her the best goddamn dinner of her life and then take her home and make crazy, hot fucking love to her? Have you ever done that?"

I didn't need to answer.

He looked at me intently, and then: "Why haven't you written a novel yet?" His tone was demanding, almost angry.

"A novel is a lot of work," I said simply.

"Dude, seventy hours a week of mergers and acquisitions is a lot of work," he said in the same angry tone. "And six months from now, no one's going to give a good goddamn about *any* of it. I mean, look what we fucking do with our lives! Doesn't it piss you off?"

"Alex," I said, growing weary, "yeah, sure, I'd love to write a novel, or do something risky and spontaneous. But time is limited and you can't do everything. You have to make choices. I wanted to do other things, too. Like go to college and get a good job, and do that for a while. Then graduate school. All those things take time."

"Exactly," he said, sitting forward again. "They take time

away. You graduate from college at twenty-one, you get your job, you bust your ass trying to do well, maybe go back to school, then work hard some more, and the next thing you know you're thirty-five and your fucking hair is falling out!"

I was quiet.

He looked away, shaking his head, his frustration seeming to intensify even as he vented. Then, cryptically: "It's this goddamn city."

"What do you mean?"

"I mean look at the way we live. It's ridiculous. Our friends in other cities, even our friends out in Jersey and Westchester, have normal lives. They have houses. They have wives. They have kids. A guy I work with who's *younger* than me has three kids. The oldest is *eleven*! An eleven-year-old kid!"

"Do you *want* an eleven-year-old kid, Alex?"

"No! That's not the point."

"Then what is the point?"

"The point is this city fucks with your head! I mean, it's crazy! Wacked! We live exactly the way we did in college, Jack. Instead of going to class we go to work. We still drink with our friends in crowded bars. We still chase pussy. We live in tiny apartments that are basically dorm rooms. Hell, you don't even have a bed! You're thirty-five years old and you sleep on the goddamn *floor*!"

I felt my face burn.

"You see what I'm saying?" he went on, his eyes angry and demanding. "The *point,* Jack, is that we're not twenty-one anymore, or twenty-six or even thirty! We're thirty-fucking-five!"

I had nothing to say. Nothing of any merit or consequence, anyway. And, besides, by now I was exhausted. I swallowed another mouthful of soda, then gave a listless shrug. "Like I said, Alex, time is limited and we've made our choices. Ultimately you have to accept that."

He sank back in his chair, folding his arms across his chest like a scolded child.

"I mean, like you always say," I continued, "if you spend your whole life worrying about what you haven't had time to do, you'll just make yourself miserable and ruin what time you do have."

His eyes narrowed, his lips pursed; I could see that, however reluctantly, he was wrestling with what I was saying.

"It's the same for all of us," I said. "It's not just you."

He looked hard at me for a long moment and then, once again, out into the street. He sat quietly as before, watching the people pass by, staring at them, his eyes mournful and tense, following individuals or small groups for several seconds at a time, watching them, studying them, as if he expected to see something, some tiny part of whatever he was looking for, whatever he had lost, in their appearance, their expressions, their manner, in the snippets of their conversations he was able to catch as they passed. Then, suddenly, he reached for his beer and drained the last quarter of the glass in one swallow. Setting the empty glass on the table, he gave two or three curt nods. "Right," he said abruptly. "You're right."

"Two more, guys?" our waitress asked with another bright smile.

I looked at Alex, raised my eyebrows.

"No, it's late," he said, checking his watch. "Have to be at the office early."

"Big day?" I said, trying to be light, sympathetic.

He shook his head, frowning. "Just a lot going on."

As I made my way home, a strange, weary, creeping sort of sadness overtook me. The fresh, spring-like breeze had turned chilly, and the darkness, the starless New York sky, the very night itself, seemed to push in hard around me. I didn't want to go home, but I had nowhere else to go.

Back in my apartment, I checked my hair in the mirror.

Chapter 15

The next day I met Tom for lunch. Back from his honey-moon, he was in New York for the day—dispatched from Chicago to attend to some whining client, who, conveniently enough, was also footing the bill for his coddling. "Expense account," he said, chuckling into the phone. "You know a good place?"

I arrived a few minutes late. Spotting me, Tom smiled broadly, hurried in my direction, his hand stuck out.

I was startled. "Look at you!" I erupted, almost despite myself.

Tom laughed. "I know. I was a lobster a few days ago, but it's faded to mostly tan now."

I shook my head. "No, no, it's more than that. You look . . . I don't know, you look . . . different."

"What?" he said, grinning self-consciously, his big Irish head drawn back on his neck. "I look *married*?"

"Well, yeah, I guess." I laughed. "There's a certain . . ."—

I groped for words—". . . air of legitimacy. A look of con-summation."

"Well, thank God for that!"

At the table, he pulled out pictures of the honeymoon.

"Looks like you had fabulous weather," I said, thumbing through the prints.

"We really did. Of course, I was constantly in danger of getting scorched, slopping sunscreen on every ten minutes. The Caribbean is a friggin' microwave this time of year." He shrugged good-naturedly. "But Michelle loves the beach, so what're you gonna do?"

Go somewhere else, I thought. Instead I smiled and said, "Sounds like everything went perfectly."

"It really did," he sighed with a sort of wistful amaze-ment. "The wedding went off without a hitch. The honey-moon was great. We're all moved into the new apartment. A few boxes still to unpack."

"And married life suits you?"

"So far, so good," he said. Then, right on cue: "You oughta give it a try."

Getting married, I've noticed, is like moving to Brooklyn: once your friends do it, they want you to do it too.

Then, leaning toward me over the table, he said, "I haven't told you the best part." He gave a guilty grimace. "I'm not supposed to say anything, so keep this under your hat for a while." Pause. "Michelle's pregnant."

"*What!*"

He nodded, grinning broadly. "She took one of those home tests last week and it was positive. Went to the doctor on Saturday, and sure enough—I'm gonna be a daddy." A goofy laugh. "Can you believe that?"

I was reeling; completely stunned. "*No!* No, I really can't! I mean . . ." Suddenly realizing my reaction was hardly enthusiastic or supportive, I struggled to get hold of myself. "Well . . . shit, congratulations!" I stretched out my hand. Tom grasped it tightly, beaming. I couldn't help an awkward chuckle. "It's just that . . . I mean, *good grief!* You got married less than a *month* ago!"

"It only takes once," he said. "You've heard of honeymoon babies."

"Yeah, but—" Then it occurred to me. "Oh," I groaned, "it's the birth-control thing, isn't it? You're not . . . using birth control."

He shook his head. "No, it's not that. I mean, yes, you know my position on the subject. But that's not it at all." He shrugged. "Michelle and I are both thirty-four. We've been working for ten years. We've got the money, and it's what we want."

Just then, his gaze left me and drifted out over the restaurant. His expression flattened, his eyes emptied, and for a moment he seemed very far away. Watching him, I wondered if the stunning reality of his situation—his ever so recent marriage and, three weeks later, the ludicrous fact of his impending fatherhood—had suddenly thrown or even frightened him. But a moment later, his eyes swung back to me, sparkling with anticipation, his face drawn up in a wry, easy smile, his cheeks bunched, lips curved at the corners.

He shrugged again, playfully, fearlessly. "It's time."

• • •

Nine-thirty at night, and I was exhausted.

A hellish week at work, the burden of my simmering anxiety, and now the soothing pitch and roll of the subway car as

I rode uptown had combined to produce a major Sominex effect. I could barely keep my eyes open.

Putting my head back, I closed my eyes, confident I could allow myself to linger at the brink of sleep and yet not miss my stop. Moments later, I jolted awake in a flailing, spastic twitch. Embarrassed, I quickly scanned the car: if anyone had seen my ridiculous convulsion, no one seemed to care.

As I looked around, I noticed that the woman seated directly across the car from me was reading *The Sun Also Rises*. I was surprised. It's a wonderful book, one of my favorites. But it's not every day that you see a twenty-something reading Hemingway on the subway. I studied the woman as she read, wondering who she was and what she thought of the story.

Suddenly, a passage from one of Hemingway's short stories bubbled into my mind. I stiffened, stunned by its random appearance and its potential relevance to my nagging quandary. I couldn't recall the passage specifically, but knew it was some pronouncement, some declarative statement, on the topic of women and sex.

I speed-walked home from the subway station. If anyone were to have something useful, something uniquely insightful, to say on the subject, it would be Hemingway, the great artist and world-class womanizer. The man definitely had his data.

Pushing open the door to my apartment, I dropped my briefcase and headed for the bookshelf. I pulled out my copy of Hemingway's stories, checked the table of contents, and turned to "Fathers and Sons." After a few minutes of skimming paragraphs and turning pages, I found the passage.

Nick Adams, thirty-eight years old in the story, is driving a car, his young son asleep on the seat beside him, thinking about his own father. He recalls that his father, long dead now, had been as useless on the subject of women and sex as he had been helpful teaching Nick how to fish and shoot:

> ... and Nick was glad that it had been that way; for some-one has to give you your first gun or the opportunity to get it and to use it, and you have to live where there is game or fish if you are to learn about them. .... While for the other, that his father was not sound about, all the equipment you will ever have is provided and each man learns all there is for him to know about it without advice; and it makes no difference where you live.

I dropped into my rocking chair. Knowing how precisely Hemingway wrote, and of the notoriously vast and tumultuous experience from which he no doubt was drawing, I read the passage over and over, studying the deliberate selection and placement of every word.

Finally, my eyes, my mind, focused on two words: *for him*. They seemed to stick out, breaking the rhythm of the sentence, calling attention to themselves: signal flags waving on the deck of a ship; Mona Lisa with a flower in her hair—it must have been intentional.

I removed the words and read the sentence, then replaced them and read it again. And as I read and re-read, removing and replacing, it became clear that the two small words, bland and seemingly insignificant, change the meaning of the statement entirely. Without them, the sentence would imply that complete knowledge and understanding are not only possible but easily attainable—*and each man learns all there is to know about it without advice*. With them, Hemingway seemed to be saying that on the subject of women and sex, there is only so much a man will ever understand—*and each man learns all there is for him to know about it without advice.* . . .

Raising my eyes from the page, it occurred to me that my father might be a very wise man.

Chapter 16

Returning to my office after a meeting the next afternoon, I found my message light blinking.

"Dude, I've got tix to the Yankees game tonight." Alex. Great seats, he said. Client can't make it. "Call me."

• • •

It's impossible to be unhappy at a baseball game. The bright lights, the deep green and pumpkin orange of the diamond, the easy pace of the game, the familiar rhythm, the sounds and smells, all conspire to soothe and lift the soul.

The seats were indeed fantastic—just behind the Yankee dugout along the first-base line. Alex and I ate hot dogs and drank beer. Every now and then, a foul ball looped in our direction, causing a brief surge of excitement. At the top of the sixth, when the grounds guys came out to comb the infield, we stood with everyone else and did the Village People's "YMCA" dance.

"So how's it going with Karen?" I asked as we settled back into our seats. She and Alex had gotten together two or three more times.

"Pretty good, I guess."

I looked over at him. "Just pretty good?"

He frowned. "We haven't closed the deal yet."

"*Really?*" I said, genuinely surprised. Maybe Karen *had* taken our little chat to heart. Or at least was experimenting. "It's been almost two weeks," I said. "That must be a record for you."

He shrugged. "She's making me work for it."

Turning my gaze out over the field again, I thought: she goes down on the guy the night she meets him, then plays the Blessed Virgin. Bait and switch, baby! Pick and roll! "Maybe she doesn't like bald guys," I teased.

"Not funny," he said. Then: "I'm not worried about it. She'll eventually do the right thing."

I laughed to myself. *Do the right thing.* I loved the normative thrust of the expression. As if it would be wrong, unprincipled, even *immoral* for her to deny him the pleasure of adding another notch to his belt.

But there was something else. Something even more astounding about his comment—the word "eventually." Alex still had his demands, his expectations, but was now apparently willing to wait to have them fulfilled. He had conceded the timing to Karen. This was new.

"Talked to Sarah?" he asked.

"No," I said. No further explanation. Alex didn't press it.

The game remained tied into the bottom of the eleventh when Jeter came to the plate with runners at first and second, one out. The count went two and two. The stadium was chaos as the crowd begged for a game-winning hit.

I sensed the heat. Apparently, Jeter did, too: with a quick, explosive swing, he unloaded on a knee-high fastball, launching it toward right center. The crowd erupted, leapt to its feet, arms fanning the air. The center fielder was on his horse, sprinting toward the wall. The ball reached the apex of its majestic flight, seemed to hover for a moment, then dropped. Running at full stride, head turned, the fielder reached up, snatched the ball, and crashed into the cushioned wall. The crowd heaved a collective groan as Jeter pulled up from his sprint past first and jogged stoically back to the dugout.

But the crowd remained on its feet: Jeter's near home run had allowed the runner on second to tag and move to third. With two outs, runners now on first and third, Bernie Williams came to the plate.

Again the crowd tripled the decibel level. Bernie let the first pitch sail by, earning a strike. He swung at the next two, fouling both.

The tension was unbearable—one more strike would strand two runners, one in easy scoring position, in the bottom of the eleventh. As Bernie stepped into the box and raised his bat, the crowd was screaming.

The windup . . . the delivery . . . *fastball*! Bernie swung hard. A whiff! Strike three! *No!* He caught a piece of it! A squib!

The ball dribbled, bunt-like, up the first-base line. The pitcher and first baseman both lunged toward it. The runner on third shot toward home. The catcher straddled the plate.

The pitcher reached the ball first, just as Bernie flew by on his way to first. Seizing the ball with his bare hand, the pitcher spun, threw home . . . *too late!* The runner crossed! Game over! Yankees win! Yankees win!

The crowd exploded. The Yankees tore out of the dugout and mobbed Williams. Alex and I high-fived each other and everyone else within reach. Strangers embraced. Beer flew. Over the continuing roar, Sinatra crooned: "Start spreadin' the news. . . ."

The D train back to Manhattan was a near riot, our car packed with shouting, singing, drunken fans. I looked over at Alex. He was frowning.

"What's wrong with you?"

He shook his head. "Baseball is a stupid game."

"*What?*"

"It doesn't make any sense."

"What are you talking about?"

"Dude, Jeter crushes the ball, sends it four hundred feet in the air, and gets nothing out of it. Bernie comes up, barely makes contact, rolls the ball twenty feet, earns a base hit, and wins the game. Stupid."

"It's *not* stupid!" I objected.

"Yes, it is. It's not logical," he said, shaking his head again. "It makes no sense."

"That's the *beauty* of it!" I said, horrified by his apostasy. "That it's not just about talent and skill. That it's also about luck and uncertainty. Drama and mystery. That's wha—"

I froze. I couldn't believe what I'd just said. Dropping my glance to the grimy floor of the train, I ran the notion through once more, making the connection, coming to terms with the lesson.

Looking up, I grinned at my frowning friend. "That's what makes it fun."

· · ·

When I got home, I had a message from Kim.

She was sorry, she said. She'd been thinking about it and had decided that confronting me at the restaurant wasn't fair. She'd overreacted. Maybe I had planned the date before she and I had met that Friday night, and maybe I had felt obliged to follow through. In any case, she was sure that there was more to what happened than she understood. She wanted to talk.

Her voice was calm and even—more straightforward, more sober, more coldly rational than I'd ever heard from her before.

"I love you, Jack," she said into the machine. "We can work this out."

I never returned the call.

· · ·

The next morning I phoned Janie at the office. Following a few meaningless pleasantries, I asked two or three leading questions about Sarah, tipping my hand. Janie provided informative answers. No knowing tone, no sarcasm.

"She's a terrific girl," she said finally.

"Why didn't you tell me about her before?"

"Well, until recently you weren't available. And neither was Sarah."

"She was seeing someone?"

"Three-year relationship," Janie said. "Ended very suddenly. Matt and I were shocked. We were expecting a different sort of announcement."

"Really," I said, suddenly feeling bad for Sarah. But, also, oddly relieved.

"She was pretty upset for a while," Janie continued. "But

she's bounced back. She's a very strong girl. Very sure of herself. I'm glad she's getting back out there."

"So, she's been dating?"

Janie's tone changed slightly, but noticeably. "She's a winner, Jack," she said. "Smart, beautiful, and knows who she is. A rare commodity. They don't last."

I hesitated another moment, but then: "Do you have her number at work?"

. . .

I got her voice mail and hung up.

Ten seconds later I called again and left a brief, mealy-mouthed message. Just calling to see how she was doing, I said. Was wondering if maybe she'd like to get together sometime? A drink, maybe a bite to eat? Casual, no big deal, I said.

Ridiculous, of course, under the circumstances, but there was no way, under the circumstances, not to sound ridiculous. In fact, the task at hand may well have been to sound ridiculous—to indicate that I was willing to make a fool of myself in order to earn a second chance. Returning the receiver to the cradle, I left my hand on the phone for a moment, as if to give the message time to take.

Hours passed. Totally distracted, I got almost nothing done.

At six-forty that evening, my phone rang. Sarah's voice was friendly but weary. Distant. Sorry, she said. Meetings all afternoon. Long day.

"No reason to apologize," I said, trying to be cheerful. "I understand, of course."

"Jack, I appreciate the call and the invitation. But I really . . . well, I'd rather not."

I felt my insides deflate.

"After what happened," she went on, "I think it would be best if we didn't see each other."

I wanted to hang up, just end the agony, but felt I had to say something. "Well, I'm disappointed."

"I know," she said gently. "Listen, I don't mean to be . . . I just think that for both of us . . . this makes the most sense."

Chapter 17

"Can't say I blame her," Alex said.

Saturday morning. We were shooting baskets at the playground courts on Columbus Avenue at Seventy-seventh Street. I stood under the basket, feeding the ball back to Alex.

"So what am I supposed to do now?"

"Depends on your objective."

"My objective is another chance with her. To get her to go out with me again."

"Why should she? Based on the evidence, she's made a perfectly reasonable decision not to see you." He launched another shot from twenty feet. The resulting swish through the net felt like some karma-guided affirmation of his statement.

"I had some issues, all right?" I said lamely, tossing the ball back. "Distractions. Things I had to figure out. And besides, she likes me. You said so."

"That was before she found out about your issues."

"Look," I said, feeling persecuted, "I got beaten up by Kim and was in a selfish mood for a while. Is that so terrible? So hard to understand? I mean, Janie told me that Sarah just broke up with some guy. She has to be able to understand what I've been going through."

Alex eyed me. "So you're beyond all that now."

"Yes."

"You've seen the light."

"Absolutely."

"You admit you've been a complete idiot."

I glared at him, then conceded. "Yes."

Satisfied, Alex resumed his dribbling, eyeing another shot. "Well, then you have to talk to her. You have to tell her you're sorry. Tell her how your friend Alex has been pleading with you to extricate your head from your ass, but that you were enjoying the view so much you ignored him."

He launched the shot—nothing but net.

"Fine," I said, shoving the ball back at him. "How do I tell her all that if she won't see me?"

"Well, that's the challenge, Hemingway. That's the hurdle she's set for you to clear."

"So you think this is intentional? That it's some kind of test?"

A sideways grin. "You know what's happening here. She's screening."

"What do you mean?"

He stopped dribbling. "You don't answer the phone every time it rings, right? Sometimes you screen. You wait to see who it is, or how important the message is, before you pick up. Not everyone makes the cut. Most you let go to the machine and get back to them later."

"Okay, so?"

"So, you had a priority position with Sarah. Initially. She was interested and paying attention. She took your calls and was happy to get them. But then you went waving your issues around. Wallowing in self-pity. Getting naked with your ex. You blew your favored position. You don't make the cut anymore. You're back in the pack with the maybe-laters. Or, after what happened, the probably-nevers. You've got to come up with something to make her pick up again."

He fired another shot. I caught the ball as it dropped through the hoop, then held it a moment, thinking. "Maybe I could get Janie to talk to her for me."

"Oh, that's bold," he japed.

"Well, she won't see me, and Janie lives with her brother. They're practically in-laws."

"Jack, the point of the exercise is to impress her. Not to add to the growing list of reasons why you're a loser."

I shoved the ball back at him. "You're right. I have to do it myself." Again I pondered. "Maybe I should write her a letter."

"Lame," he groaned. "What are we, sixth graders?" Then, in a funny, mocking voice: "If you maybe still like me, check this box."

"Okay, fine. I'll leave a message on her voice mail. That way she can listen at her convenience. When she's ready."

Alex stopped dribbling again; held the ball between his forearm and hip. "A voice-mail message?"

I nodded. "It'll be me, in my own words, and yet it's respectful of her time and feelings. It's acknowledging her position. Her point of view. It's, you know"—I groped for words—"validating of her station."

Alex looked at me as if I were from outer space. "Validating of her station?"

"Yes."

Again he stared. "What rock do you live under?" I opened my mouth to protest, but was cut off. "Dude, women don't want their fucking stations validated. Whatever the hell that means. They want passion. Romance. Remember what we talked about at the gym a couple weeks ago?"

I'd had enough of the sarcasm and abuse. "Yeah, I remember, Alex. Women want to be seized. And dragged around by the hair."

"That's right."

"Taken! By force if necessary!"

"Exactly."

I was angry now. "That's great advice, Alex. Just great. You know, maybe I'll go stake out her apartment. She has to come out at some point, right? And when she does, I'll be there. Waiting, like some obsessed stalker."

"Maybe you should."

"Grab her in my arms and *force* her to listen."

"Exactly. Make an impression."

"Oh, yes, *absolutely*! That'll impress her!"

Alex cocked his head, leveling a speculative glance on me. "Jack, Sarah is a sexy, smart, very cool chick. She has options. You think that just because you've come to your senses and are suddenly interested that she should still be interested in you? That just because you want her, you somehow *deserve* her? Lots of men probably want a shot at her. Janie said she was dating, right?"

I said nothing.

"The question now, my romantically challenged friend, is how *badly* do you want her?" He stepped forward, sticking a finger in my chest. "What are *you* willing to do? Exactly how far are *you* willing to go? That's what she wants to know. That's the challenge. And it's a question only you can answer."

"Yes, but I can't—"

"You're the writer, for chrissake!" he said, his face knotted with frustration. "Do something dramatic!"

"Fine! But I can't just—"

"Yes, you *can*!"

"Alex, you're not being realistic!"

"Jack!"

"*Alex!*"

Suddenly dropping the basketball, he lunged forward and seized me by the upper arms. "Sarah, listen to me!" he said desperately, his face only inches from mine. "One minute, that's all I'm asking! Just hear me out! One minute!" He stepped into me, seizing me in his arms, one wrapped tightly around my waist, the other around my back. Thrusting himself against me, I was tipped backward, off balance, helpless in his grasp. I pushed vainly at his shoulders, but he only pulled me tighter. "I'm not a perfect man, Sarah," he went on, "but I'm enough of one to admit when I've made a mistake. And I've made a mistake, Sarah. A *terrible* mistake! I've been an idiot. Selfish and blind. I've let my pain and fear cloud my judgment."

Stunned, I was rigid in his grasp, my head drawn back stiffly, eyes wide with horror.

"You can't see these things coming, Sarah," he continued in the same desperate tone. "You can't plan them. They happen at the strangest times. I wasn't ready when you suddenly appeared. But I'm ready for you now. I can't stop thinking about you. You're the most *beautiful,* the most *exciting*"— he squeezed me tighter with each emphasized word—"the *sexiest* woman I've *ever* met! I don't blame you for thinking I'm a prick. But if you can somehow find it in your heart to give me another chance, I'll show you the kind of man I can be. The kind of man I *really* am."

Still clutching me, Alex stared deeply into my eyes, his expression rapturous passion. For a moment, I was sure he would kiss me. Then, just as suddenly, he released me, stepped back, casually picked up the basketball, turned, and fired a true shot.

Chapter 18

I spent the rest of the weekend alone: pacing my apartment, sitting in my rocking chair, channel surfing, spitting obscenities.

Saturday night, I ordered in Chinese, tried to read but couldn't, fell into a grainy sleep in front of a Bette Davis movie. My coffee run late Sunday morning was my first venture out in nearly twenty-four hours. Like some newly emerged hermit, I blinked my eyes against the glare of the outside world.

Ensconced again in my hovel—and that's exactly what my apartment had become—I sipped the acquired coffee while paging mindlessly through the Sunday *Times*. For nearly two hours my eyes dutifully floated over line after line of carefully wrought, preposterously informative prose— all the news that's fit to print—but absorbed practically nothing. Worn out from thinking and puzzling, my tired brain numb and throbbing, I simply couldn't concentrate, couldn't focus, anymore. And having accomplished exactly nothing during my daylong confinement, I couldn't stand to be alone anymore, but knew I couldn't bear the company of anyone else either.

I was a mess.

Feeling cooped up and at loose ends, I decided I needed a walk. I tossed the paper in the corner, grabbed my keys (after a brief search) and headed for the door.

I found myself in Central Park, wandering south down the western slope of the loop. It was a magnificent late-summer day, wide and warm, and New York City's backyard was jammed. Joggers huffed along in their pinch-faced rush, while couples strolled leisurely, some arm in arm, some pushing baby carriages, others clinging tightly, as if sharing a final desperate embrace. Dogs tested their leashes, joyfully barking and sniffing, beside themselves to finally be out of their masters' kennel-like apartments. Bikers and rollerbladers careened insanely down the long, meandering stretch of the hill, the thrill of speed and freedom—a rare sensation in Manhattan—numbing any sense of fear or even caution. Sales were brisk at the pushcart ice cream and soda vendors.

Out on the lake, dozens of battered blue rowboats lazily drifted like so many dragonflies buzzing over the murky surface of a neighborhood pond. Hearing a woman's sudden shrieking laugh, I spotted a couple nuzzling in the back of one of the tiny crafts as it precariously tipped and wobbled.

Farther down the hill, the lower meadow was a vast, throbbing sprawl of urban humanity—what looked to be thousands of people in ludicrous proximity engaged in every kind of playful activity and yet, somehow, peacefully sharing the twenty-acre area. Turning off the paved road of the lower loop, I plunged in, carefully stepping around blankets, bodies, and otherwise occupied plots of grassy ground: dozing sunbathers lay blissfully bronzing; kids ran screaming, chasing dogs and each other; lovers flew kites and groped under trees; footballs, baseballs, and Frisbees were tossed, soccer balls and Hackey Sacks kicked, wiffle, paddle, and volley balls batted; amateur radicals sat tattooed and earrings dangling in circles of four, five, and six, strumming secondhand guitars and passing marijuana pipes; gay men, oiled and watchful, posed on beach towels along the north fence line, their bikini briefs brashly flaunting their wares and drawing chuckles from others nearby; tattered, homeless-looking characters wandered randomly amid the crush, hauling bulging knapsacks and calling, "Ice-cold beer and soda!" All this under the watchful gaze of towering midtown. It was the last weekend of summer and it seemed the entire city had turned out to pay tribute.

I made my way to a neglected spot of shade beneath the exploding leaves of a giant elm on the edge of the meadow, where, giving in to long-suppressed impulses, I simply stretched out in the warm grass, crossing my legs at the ankles, my fingers on my chest. Gazing up through the branches to the otherwise open, unobstructed sky, I thought I might be absolutely anywhere on earth except the middle of Manhattan. I closed my eyes, breathed deeply, wearily, and, with a fresh September breeze swirling cool around me, tried to clear my head and relax.

When I woke up, the meadow was nearly empty and the sun was headed down.

Chapter 19

At work the next morning, my mood hadn't changed much. I'd managed to focus enough to move a few things off my desk, but by midmorning had exhausted the energy required to hold off thoughts of my dilemma. I soon found myself slumped in my chair, chin on my fist, feet propped across the rim of the wastebasket.

It wasn't that I suddenly knew what to do. There was no epiphany. No fog-piercing moment of clarity. It wasn't even that things made slightly more sense. It was that I'd simply had enough. I was tired of being confused. Tired of endlessly thinking and puzzling and getting nowhere. And tired most of all of what this single aspect of my existence was doing to the rest of my life.

And my arrival at that significant if rather vague resolution provided just enough focus for an even more remarkable realization to form—that the world, my world, had changed

in stunning and profound ways: I didn't love Kim anymore;
Tom was married and would soon be a father; Alex was
losing his hair and was perilously close to relationship status
with Karen. *Major shit was going down!*

I remember slowly shaking my head as I moved from one
astonishing notion to another. In fact, calling it all to mind as
I sat there slumped at my desk, I found it almost, quite frankly,
too much to comprehend. It was as if, without our even realizing, events had somehow overtaken us all—our lives playing out the scenes of a bizarre story line that had little if
anything to do with who we'd always thought we were. I suddenly had the feeling I sometimes experience at a movie theater when, returning from a quick trip to the men's room or
concession stand, I find that the film has shifted onto a trajec-
tory so different, so incomprehensible, that after several minutes of struggle I'm finally forced to lean over to whomever
I'm with to whisper helplessly, "What did I miss?"

Just after eleven, I sat up, reached for the phone, and dialed Information. The address provided, I stood and grabbed
my suit jacket.

"I have some things to take care of," I told my secretary.
"I'll be back in half an hour or so."

Outside on the sidewalk, I walked briskly, weaving through
the late-morning foot traffic, hustling across intersections to
beat flashing "Don't Walk" signs. I had to do it before I talked
myself out of it. Before reason and caution reclaimed me.

The building was standard Sixth Avenue fare—a monstrous, up-ended shoebox of steel and glass. I pushed through
the revolving doors, walked across the marbled lobby to the
corporate directory mounted on the opposite wall, then headed
for the elevators.

Delivered to the twenty-sixth floor, I found the names of the founding members etched in ornate lettering on an elegant glass entryway . . . and one of those magnetic access contraptions mounted on the wall. But luck was on my side: just as I approached the entrance, appropriately dressed and looking altogether as if I belonged, a woman happened to push through the glass door and let me pass behind her—actually holding the door open for me. A mere interloper, I was in.

The reception area was large and tastefully plush: a paisley-patterned sofa and loveseat positioned around a darkly stained oval coffee table; fresh flowers; the week's magazines; the day's newspaper; and a receptionist's desk—but, oddly, no receptionist. Turning to my left, toward what appeared to be the heart of the office, I walked down a long hallway until I came upon a secretary typing at her desk.

"Excuse me," I said, "I'm looking for Sarah Mitchell."

The woman looked up, eyeing me with polite suspicion. "Is she expecting you?"

"Not really," I said, looking around on the off chance I might spot her. "But I'm a friend."

Blinking discreetly, the woman forced a pleasant but frosty smile as she reached for the telephone. "Your name?"

"Jack Lafferty."

Just then, my eye was caught by motion to my left. Turning, I was astonished to see Sarah tugging open and then disappearing behind a door farther down the hallway.

"Thank you, I see her." With that, I headed for the door.

"Excuse me, *sir*!" the secretary called behind me. "Sir, you can't—"

Ignoring her, I continued my flight down the hall, thrilled at yet another stroke of luck: I didn't want my presence an-

nounced; I wanted to surprise Sarah, deliver the message before she had time to harden her mind and heart. This was the
moment. Luck was with me. The tightness in my stomach
felt right.

"*Sir!*"

Glancing quickly over my shoulder, I saw that the secretary had scurried from behind her desk and was now chasing
me down the hallway.

I didn't stop. I marched on, propelled by a new purpose,
a new conviction, and determined to act before it left me.
Do something dramatic! *Seize the carp!* Reaching the door
through which Sarah had passed, I gave two sharp knocks,
pushed it open, walked into the room . . .

. . . and froze.

The room was large, with four long tables positioned one
behind the other from the head of the room to the rear—a
classroom. At the tables sat about thirty people, all in business
attire, all now staring at me. The group had apparently been
listening to a presentation of some sort being delivered by a
trim, primly suited, competent-looking woman who, rudely
interrupted by my knocking and sudden entrance, stood clearly
startled beside an overhead projector mounted on a stand.

Scanning the bemused faces of my unexpected audience, I
spotted Sarah: sitting at the third table, second from the
right, mouth agape.

Just then, the secretary who had given chase arrived at the
open doorway and, seeing the bizarre scene, also froze, her
face tight with apprehension.

The woman at the projector arched her eyebrows and,
cocking her head in mock accommodation, said, "May I help
you?"

Thoroughly flummoxed, I looked blankly at the woman, then again at the audience, including Sarah—all staring at me. "I . . . I'm sorry," I stammered. "Excuse me."

The presenter gave me a lingering look of derision before turning back to her students. I also turned and stepped toward the doorway.

"Okay," I heard her sigh behind me. "So, we were talking about—"

I whipped around. "I'm sorry."

The woman turned with a start. Interrupted in midsentence for a second time, her expression was a mix of confusion and indignation.

But my moment had come. Now was the time. I had to do it.

"I'm terribly sorry," I said again, holding up my palms in a plea for patience and understanding. "I have something . . . something very important to say to someone here."

Clearly appalled by my impertinence, the woman stared at me, her eyes wide, her face knotted.

"It'll only take a moment," I said. "And since I've already caused a disruption . . ."

At a loss for words, the woman frowned wearily and put a hand to her hip, as if to say with studied sarcasm: "Oh, by *all* means . . ."

I stiffly nodded my thanks and, lowering my hands, slowly turned to face the room of people. Shaking with nervousness, I gulped for air.

"There's someone here I owe an apology to," I began.

My eyes found Sarah across the wide room. She looked stunned, even terrified. Meanwhile, the rest of the assembled group stared back at me with a range of expressions. Some seemed to say, "Who the *hell* is this guy?" Others seemed to convey a certain amused curiosity—"This oughta be good."

The incredulous secretary continued to stand tensely in the doorway.

"I'm not going to identify the person," I said. "I've done enough damage already without embarrassing them. They know who they are."

Sarah's eyes darted nervously around the room.

"We've all done things we regret," I continued. "We've all said things or behaved in ways we're not proud of later. And sometimes the reasons for that bad behavior have nothing to do with the situation at hand. Or the person we happen to be with at the moment. We're hurt or angry or frustrated about something else entirely. Maybe something that happened days or weeks or even months before. For whatever reason we hold on to the bad feelings. We wallow in them. It's not a smart thing to do. Those bad feelings can come out at the wrong time. Maybe we'll end up doing something we'll regret later. Maybe we'll hurt someone innocent. Maybe even someone we care about."

Sarah, sitting stiffly at her place at the table, still appeared horrified.

"It's stupid," I went on. "It makes no sense. And it's totally unfair to the people we hurt. But we do it anyway. We feel entitled to do it. Someone else has upset or offended us, and we think that gives us license to be a jerk. It's perfectly human, but that doesn't make it right."

For just a moment, I noticed that the expressions of a few people in the front row had softened from a kind of hostile impatience to something more like reluctant concern. They seemed to be hearing what I was trying to say. Or maybe just felt sorry for this clown making an ass of himself.

"I behaved badly a couple of Fridays ago," I said, finally getting to the point. "I let my anger and frustration about another situation get the best of me." I paused a moment, searching for a better explanation, something more specific, more reasoned. Nothing came to mind. "Anyway, I came here today to say that I'm sorry. And to let you know that I'm usually someone of better judgment. I can't undo what happened, but I'd ask that you try to understand. And I'd like very much to make it up to you. If you're willing to let me try, I hope you'll give me a call."

The room was utterly quiet. Amazingly, the faces of the assembled attorneys had indeed softened. Despite the weirdness of the situation, or maybe because of it, they seemed to be listening, and with interest. Even the twice-interrupted presenter seemed vaguely affected.

"Thank you," I said to her. "Sorry again for the interruption."

With that, I turned and walked out of the room, stepping past the blank-faced secretary.

• • •

Out on the street again, I seemed to float down the sidewalk, the sounds of the traffic and the people around me muted into an odd underwater muffle. I wasn't sure what I had just done, but I had definitely done something. Something out of character. Something bold. Risky to the point of being rash. Even reckless.

I felt a certain heady satisfaction. A raw, depleted feeling of accomplishment, as if I'd just finished a marathon or summited a challenging peak. It was a good feeling. I had done it. Laid it all on the line. And in a way even more spectacular, more audacious, than I'd intended. In fact, I had to admit to myself that, had I known what awaited me at Sarah's firm— an audience of thirty people!—I would never have left my office.

And yet, when confronted with such a daunting obstacle, a final challenge to my resolve, I'd delivered. Somehow, for whatever reason, I'd managed to follow through. I didn't know what would come of it—what impact, if any, my performance might have on Sarah. But at least I'd done what I could. I'd said what I came to say. The rest would be up to her.

I didn't have to wait long to find out. Suddenly, from behind me: "*Jack!*"

Turning, I saw Sarah marching down the sidewalk toward me, slicing through the other pedestrians, her face taut, shoulders lowered, arms pumping as she approached in an angry speed-walk. I was bowled over—I'd never guessed she might follow me—and my astonishment, together with the ferocity of Sarah's expression, froze me in the middle of the wide sidewalk.

"Just what the hell was *that?*" she shouted, still yards away.

With nowhere to hide, I braced myself.

Brushing past the last body between us, she stopped abruptly before me, jamming her hands on her hips. "What *was* that?" she demanded, her eyes blazing with indignation.

"Sarah—"

"How could you do something like that?"

I heaved a sigh. "I just had to tell you."

"Tell me what?"

"That I'm sorry about what happened."

"You're sorry."

"Yes."

"That's the message."

"Yes."

"You couldn't *call* to tell me that?" Her tone was hard and mean.

"No."

"Why not?"

"Because calling wouldn't be enough," I said.

"Enough for what?"

"I wanted you to know that I'm sorry, but also to understand why it happened. To understand what's been happening with me. And why what happened with Kim happened." My ability to articulate coherently was breaking down; frustrated, I fumbled for words. "And what's been happening with you and me relative to what's been happening with me and Kim."

Her face pinched with exasperation. "What the hell are you talking about?"

"I've been resisting you, Sarah."

"*Resisting* me?"

"Yes! Look, it took me a long time to respond to you. To get to the point where I was willing to ask you out. Willing to let you into my life, even in the slightest way."

Her eyes flared with anger. "Oh, and you're quite sure that I was interested! *Quite* sure that I wanted into your life! *Quite* sure that I was there for the taking!"

"What, you're saying you haven't been interested? That everything that's been happening between us has just been my imagination?"

"What everything?" she demanded. "What's been happening between us, Jack? We've been on *one* date together! One date that ended miserably!"

"That's exactly what I'm saying. Nothing has really happened yet because I haven't let it. I didn't want to get involved."

"*You* didn't want to get involved?"

"That's right. I didn't want another relationship. And, frankly, I think that's part of why what happened with Kim that Friday happened."

That was more than Sarah could take. Infuriated, she raised her fists to her head, then smashed them to her sides again. "So it's *my* fault?" she shrieked. "*My* fault that you slept with your ex-fiancée?"

"That's not what I said, Sarah. I'm just explaining to you why—"

"That's *not* an explanation! That's bullshit! Self-serving, duck-the-issue, psychobabble *bull*shit!"

"No, it's not."

"It's not? It's *not*? Then what is it, Jack?"

"Sarah, please . . ."

"What the hell are you trying to say?"

"I'm trying to say I think I'm falling in love with you!" I nearly shouted.

I continue to believe the statement shocked me even more than Sarah. In fact, my declaration seemed to make no impression on her whatsoever. She didn't flinch or soften in the slightest way. Instead, she continued to stare at me with the same angry, demanding intensity; her eyes hard, shoulders square, hands planted on her hips.

Meanwhile, I was reeling. I couldn't believe that I'd said it. My face flushed; my pores opened. I felt exposed and humiliated. But despite my racing heart and shaking insides, despite Sarah's impervious expression, I knew I couldn't retreat. Standing there on Sixth Avenue, in the middle of the crowded late-morning sidewalk, people brushing by from every direction, I realized that this, and not earlier in her office, was my moment. "I can't stop thinking about you, Sarah," I said.

And then I blanked.

The force of the trauma, the heat of my searing anxiety, finally severed my cognitive connections. I couldn't think, couldn't articulate. I stood there for what seemed like hours wilting under the glare of Sarah's burning gaze.

But then, out of nowhere, Alex's basketball-court speech suddenly bubbled into my head. With nothing else to go on, with nothing to lose, I read from the script. "I wasn't ready when you suddenly appeared, Sarah. But I'm ready for you now. I can't stop thinking about you," I said again. "You're the most beautiful, the most exciting woman I've ever met." And I meant it. "I don't blame you for thinking I'm a jerk. But there were reasons, *real* reasons, for the way I behaved."

I couldn't remember any more of the speech. Standing there unprotected, unprepped, unrepresented, there was nothing left to say except the simple, honest, unaffected truth: "I want another chance with you, Sarah."

But she was unmoved. "And you thought you could impress me by pulling a stunt like that? By coming unannounced to my office? By pushing your way past a frightened secretary? Barging into a meeting and embarrassing me in front of thirty of my colleagues!"

"They don't know I was talking to you."

"You don't think they'll find out?" she shouted angrily. "After you left, the instructor, not knowing what the hell else to do, called a fifteen-minute break. And what do you think everyone started talking about? 'Who was he?' 'How did he get in?' 'Why did he do it?' 'Is he crazy?' 'Who was he talking to?' 'Obviously a woman, right?' 'A man would never do something so stupid for a male friend.'" She looked at me hard. "There were only six other women in the room, Jack, and three of them are married! They'll probably have it figured out before I even get back there!"

Finally understanding the position I'd put her in, realizing I'd probably demolished whatever slim chance I might have had, I felt the new strength, the new vitality I'd celebrated just minutes before, collapse within me. I stood there, exhausted, depleted, not knowing what to say.

"It was an incredibly selfish, *stupid* thing that you did! I don't know *what* you could have been thinking!"

I looked at the sidewalk between my shoes. "I wanted to do something dramatic," I said feebly.

Sarah gave a sharp, scowling sort of laugh. "Well, then congratulations, Jack! If drama was what you were after, you certainly succeeded!"

With that, she turned on her heel. All I could do was watch her walk away.

· · ·

Back in my office, I sat trance-like at my desk. I hadn't called Alex, or anyone else, or been able to do the first bit of work. I was numb, enveloped by an odd combination of unspeakable humiliation and profound calm—my own uniquely bizarre sort of post-traumatic disorder.

Hours passed.

Sometime late that afternoon, my secretary's head poked around the edge of my door. "Are you in?"

I looked up, bleary-eyed.

"You didn't answer your phone," she said. "Are you not taking calls?"

"My phone rang?" She nodded. Strange; I hadn't heard anything. "Who is it?"

"Someone named Sarah."

I bolted upright, reached for the phone. "Hello?" My secretary discreetly ducked out.

"Why did you want to do something dramatic?" Sarah's voice was flat and even, no discernible inflection of any kind. That, together with the odd directness of the question, paralyzed me for a moment.

"I wanted you to know how sorry I was."

"Why not just pick up the phone and tell me?"

"I didn't think something so easy would work."

"Work how? What do you mean?"

"I wanted to break through whatever barrier you'd built between us. I wanted to make an impression."

"Something doesn't have to be dramatic to be sincere, Jack. In fact, drama and sincerity are often negatively correlated."

"They weren't this time."

I heard her sigh into the phone. "Well, it was quite a performance. I'll give you that."

I cringed. "I'm sorry. . . ."

"You are?"

"Well, of course. It was . . . ridiculous. Completely crazy."

"Yes, it was."

Though alone in my office, I hid my face in my palm. "I don't know what to say, Sarah." And I didn't.

"Well, neither do I," she said in the same unreadable tone. Then: "No one's ever done anything quite like that for me."

I removed my hand. "Really?"

"Really."

"You're not angry?"

Pause. "To be honest, I'm not sure what I am," she said. "But, no, I wouldn't say that I'm angry."

Stunned, I slowly pushed back in my chair and stood up. My eyes jumped around the space of my office, as if searching for some kind of sign—any clue as to what to do or say next.

"By the way," Sarah went on, "the secretary who chased you down the hallway has assured me that my secret is safe." Then, with a little chuckle in her voice: "She also thinks you're very romantic."

I took the shot: "Any chance you'd meet me for a drink tonight?" I winced, bracing for rejection.

Another pause, this one longer. "A part of me would love to, Jack, but—"

"Could you go with that part of you?" I interrupted. "Just this once? Just tonight?" I'd been reduced to begging, but I didn't care. "You have the rest of your life to listen to the other part."

I heard her sigh into the phone. It was a sigh of reluctance, of struggling with better judgment.

"Listen," I said, "I know I'm asking a lot. You don't have to answer now. Just think about it, okay? I'll be at a place called Hennessey's at seven o'clock. It's on Fifty-third, two blocks south of your office. Join me there if you want to."

• • •

I gave Alex a quick call.

"Flowers! Candy! Maybe a piece of jewelry!"

"That's laying it on a bit thick, don't you think?"

"Jack, you're on probation! You're in purgatory! You *cannot* lay it on too thick! Tell me you at least have a great place picked out."

"We're only meeting for a drink," I said.

"Setting is everything!" he exploded. A huff of exasperation. "Why do I have to tell you these things? You're the writer!"

"I don't even know if she'll come."

"Patience, dude," he said, his voice lower, more soothing. "Even if she does show, she might make you wait awhile. I would. Just settle in. And try to relax. *Have a drink for chrissake!*"

Chapter 20

I arrived early. Seemed the wise thing to do. But Alex was right—I waited and waited. And waited.

An hour and a half, I waited. No Sarah.

And then, suddenly, I saw her. Smart navy suit, shoulder bag, her hair pulled back into a casually professional ponytail. Despite the ordeal of her day, she looked fresh and clear-eyed. Beautiful.

I gave her a wave. She smiled and headed my way. The same loose, effortless stride; the easy flow from leg to hip, arm to shoulder. This time it didn't bother me.

As she approached, I tried to imagine her with a guitar case over her shoulder. Legal eagle plays the Eagles. The contrast was magnificent. Irresistible. I felt the creature stir.

"I'm sorry, Jack," she said, with apparent sincerity. "Just as I was leaving, naturally, a client called with an emergency."

"No problem at all," I said, smiling. "I know how that can happen."

It was a Monday night and the bar was nearly empty. Tiny glassed candles flickered happily on small, round tables. Stan Getz drifted down from the ceiling. Sarah sipped red wine. A scotch and soda sat before me.

"I'm surprised you came," I said.

Sarah smiled softly. "I guess we surprised each other today."

"Why did you come?"

"I needed a drink," she said flatly. She chuckled, gave a little shrug. "Curious, I guess." She paused a moment, then: "Tell me the truth. Why did you do it?"

"I wanted to see you again, Sarah."

An eyebrow arched slightly; she was listening.

"I'm sorry about last week. It had nothing to do with you." I cringed inwardly at the sound of the old cliché. "My previous relationship ended fairly recently," I said. "And badly."

"So I gathered at the restaurant," she said.

I nodded grimly.

"Janie filled me in, too."

I feigned annoyance. "And I thought she was on my side."

"She is," Sarah said, smiling gently. Then, suddenly, she seemed pensive. "Is it really over?"

"Yes, it's over."

"She's not here, is she?" She looked quickly over both shoulders.

I gave a frowning sort of smile. "No, she's not here. I searched the room carefully."

Sarah's mouth twisted; she paused. "Any second thoughts?"

"None."

She studied me, then nodded. "To be honest, Jack," she said, "I know what you've been going through. I was in a relationship that ended not too long ago."

"I heard," I said.

Now Sarah frowned. "And I thought Janie was on my side."

"She is," I said, and we both laughed at Janie's apparent skill as a double agent.

She shared a bit of the story with me. The specifics were unique, but the theme was universal—two people who, for whatever reason, just couldn't make each other happy. As I listened, the sad familiarity began to weigh on me. Suddenly uncertain, my mind drifted.

"I'm boring you," I heard her say.

I looked up. "No, sorry. What you were saying just reminded me of something else."

"What?"

I shook my head. "It's stupid."

"Tell me."

"Actually it's kind of weird."

"*Tell* me," she said, leaning toward me threateningly.

I hesitated, and then: "Spandex."

"You were thinking about *spandex*?"

"Just sort of popped into my head."

Sarah's eyes narrowed. "You don't own any, do you?"

"No, why?"

"I'm glad you don't."

Suddenly she had my undivided attention. "Why?"

"I don't know," she said. "Just don't like men in spandex. Hard to explain."

"John Wayne never wore spandex," I said.

A knowing smile: "Exactly."

"Of course, I'm no John Wayne."

Sarah was quiet for a moment. "Jack is a nickname for John, right?"

I nodded.

"So your first name is John," she said. "That's a start."

"How so?"

"John is a good, solid, masculine name," she said. "I hate when men have names like Leslie, or Carroll, or . . ."

"Or Dana," I said.

She laughed. "Or Dana."

I sipped at my drink.

"Thought you gave it up."

"Abstinence doesn't work," I said. "I'm taking a new approach. Moderation. Alex tells me that a little every day is even good for you."

"He's right," she said. "It's good for your heart."

I looked at her hard, straight on. "So what do you say?"

Sarah returned my gaze without blinking or flinching. "Well . . . what have we got to lose?"

I smiled, gave a careless shrug. "Sanity. Self-respect. Dignity. Time. Money."

Sarah frowned; bit her lip. "Hmmm," she intoned, playing along. "And what would we have to gain?"

I thought for a moment. "Potentially," I said, "companionship. Satisfaction. Contentment. A sense of completeness." I paused, then said it: "Passion."

Again she held my glance, then leaned toward me over the table. "Well," she said softly, taking my hand, "that all sounds pretty good."

I continued to look at her. She was lovely: her brown hair tucked behind one ear, head tilted slightly, her green eyes open and inviting. Unafraid.

"Yeah," I heard myself say, suddenly feeling new and free. Willing somehow, even hopeful. "Actually, it does."

. . .

There is a light that hovers over Manhattan at night—a bright, expansive, incandescent glow that seems to float somewhere between the top of the city and the sky. On clear nights the light is there, but is thinner and more vague—you almost miss it. But on nights when the sky is cloudy, the light is broad and brilliant as the soft, ruffled opacity of the clouds, reflecting and refracting the electric energy from thousands of apartments and offices and restaurants and bars below, crowns the city with a kind of halo. On nights like these the city does not seem smaller or to crouch as one might expect, but in fact seems taller, more spectacular, more audacious than ever—as the reaching spires quite literally scrape the sky.